W

This man – this stranger, with his unusual scent – had done as she did. He'd gone from human to beast, changing his form in the blink of an eye.

For er entire life, Raven had believed she was an an y, a freak of nature. The only one.

Nov e appearance of this stranger proved she wa . The fact that she'd witnessed his change me: he was no longer alone.

She ot used to a solitary existence. While she wo 't call living in a cave comfortable, it felt sa nd loneliness wasn't something she often th t of. And yet the very possibility of another li : – half wolf, half human – was tantalising.

Available in August 2010
from Mills & Boon® Nocturne™

The Highwayman
by Michele Hauf

Wild Wolf
by Karen Whiddon

Shadow of the Vampire
by Meagan Hatfield

KAREN WHIDDON

Wild·Wolf

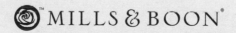

MILLS & BOON

First published in Great Britain 2010
Harlequin Mills & Boon Limited,
Eton House, 18-24 Paradise Road, Richmond, Surrey TW9 1SR

© Karen Whiddon 2009

ISBN: 978 0 263 88772 3

89-0810

Harlequin Mills & Boon policy is to use papers that are natural, renewable and recyclable products and made from wood grown in sustainable forests. The logging and manufacturing processes conform to the legal environmental regulations of the country of origin.

Printed and bound in Spain
by Litografia Rosés S.A., Barcelona

Karen Whiddon started weaving fanciful tales for her younger brothers at the age of eleven. Amidst the Catskill Mountains of New York, then the Rocky Mountains of Colorado, she fuelled her imagination with the natural beauty of the rugged peaks and spun stories of love that captivated her family's attention.

Karen now lives in North Texas, where she shares her life with her very own hero of a husband and three doting dogs. Also an entrepreneur, she divides her time between the business she started and writing the contemporary romantic suspense and paranormal romances that readers enjoy. You can e-mail Karen at KWhiddon1@ aol.com or write to her at PO Box 820807, Fort Worth, Texas 76182, USA. Fans of her writing can also check out her website, www.KarenWhiddon.com.

To those wounded and wild souls. If you're alone,
I hope you find your other half soon.

Chapter 1

"Another Feral shifter." Hanging up the phone, Simon Caldwell dragged his hand across his face and tried to smile at his fellow Protector and friend, Anton Beckham, known as Beck. "There's been a murder—a professor up at CU, in Boulder. They think a Feral killed him, so it's another search and destroy. The Feral's been located—living up on a nearby mountain. Your assignment, this time." There was more—much more, but Beck would receive that info in the case file.

Beck frowned. "Doesn't the Council realize

how burned out I am? Hellhounds, I had to eliminate my last three."

"Let me talk to Ross." Simon should have seen this coming. Burnout. All the telltale signs were there. "I'll take the job. You need a break."

"You've killed your last seven," Beck pointed out. "If anyone should have burnout, it's you."

"I don't get burnout."

"Right," Beck said, grimacing. "You're the Terminator."

Grinning, Simon shrugged and poured himself another cup of coffee. Returning to his seat at the polished steel table, he took a long drink. "Unlike you, I don't let emotions get in the way of what I have to do."

"Emotions have nothing to do with it. One of those last three Ferals could have been rehabilitated. I know it."

"You *knew* it, huh? When did you realize you might be wrong? When he attacked you and you nearly lost your arm?"

"The Council wouldn't give me enough time," Beck insisted. "Come on, man. Show a little compassion."

Simon said nothing, knowing any further argument would be pointless. Beck knew The

Protector's Creed as well as he did. Drumming his fingers on the metal table that had always seemed more appropriate in a laboratory than a kitchen, he sipped his coffee and stared at nothing.

"You really don't give a wolf's ass, do you?" Beck sounded faintly accusatory.

"Of course I do. But let's look at the stats." Simon took a long drink from his chipped mug. "Out of the last forty-seven Ferals encountered in the past year, only six were able to be saved."

"Grim statistics, true. But you know as well as I do that some of the Protectors are trigger-happy, particularly the European and Middle Eastern contingent."

"First threatening move, you shoot." Simon hated pointing out the obvious. As soon as his friend left the room, he was going to call in a recommendation that Beck be sent on enforced medical leave. An uncertain Protector was a dead Protector. He didn't want that to happen to Beck.

"You have to give them more of a chance."

When Simon didn't comment, Beck pushed himself away from the table.

"You know what your problem is, Caldwell?"

"I'm sure you're going to tell me." Simon couldn't keep the weariness from his voice. "Let me take a wild guess. I'm too hard. Unfeeling. Too old."

"Nope," Beck said, surprising him. "You're not too old. You're only thirty-four, a year older than me. I can tell you think I shouldn't take this assignment, because you're worried I'll fail. But you've got a worse problem than I do. I think you identify too closely with the Ferals. 'Grass is greener' type of thing. That's why you terminate them so quickly. Because they scare you."

Simon snorted. "You're wrong."

"Maybe I am." Beck sounded tired. "But honestly, Simon. Sometimes you seem danger-ously close to Feral yourself."

"The end result is all that matters." Eyes narrowed, Simon slammed his mug on the drain-board. "I'll ignore your insult. This time. Remember, I'm the one the Council always calls to clean up the mess guys like you make."

Beck sighed, head in hands. "Sorry."

"I'm going to take this case," Simon told him. "Not only because you need a break, but because this seems particularly intriguing. The murdered professor is rumored to have been keeping two shifters captive for years. One of them is the Feral."

"How'd we locate this one?"

Simon knew his grin looked savage. "How do we always? Rumors of a werewolf, sightings. Thefts, appearances. Humans talk. Then finally, a shifter reports to their local council."

"What about the other Feral, the second one?"

"The Society hasn't located her yet. She's either very careful, or very lucky."

"Her?" Beck looked even more troubled now.

Simon nodded. "Two females. One—or both of them—is likely the killer."

"Kept captive? Hounds know, they had reason."

"There you go again." Shaking his head, Simon didn't bother to hide his disgust. "I'm taking this case."

"Go ahead." Beck didn't argue. Not about that. "But you know what? You're cold. Hard. I think it's time the Council should reconsider their training methods. Like taking us from our parents before we even start school." He didn't bother to hide the bitterness in his voice. "Most of us can't even remember our birth family. There's no reason."

"First off, they don't *take* us. We're given. You know that. When we exhibit skills beyond those of others our age. Our parents are *honored* to send us. You know that."

"Maybe." Beck dropped his head. "But I still think we go to training too young."

"Do you? Years of training hones our skills, inspires loyalty. In the end, none of that matters." Simon crossed his arms, weary of the same old argument. "We're born to be what we're born to be. Forgetting that is what gets you in trouble."

Pushing himself up, Beck flipped him the bird before dropping his cup in the sink. "I'm going upstairs. Do you want to make the call, or shall I?"

"I'll do it."

As soon as the other man left the room, Simon picked up the phone and dialed Ross, their unit commander. No way was he letting Beck go on this assignment. Until he got his head together, Beck was a disaster waiting to happen.

Blowing snow and biting wind made Raven shiver, despite the thick pelt gifted to her by the Old One when she died. Raven had cried when the old wolf went still, lifting her human face to howl into the night, exactly like her wolf-family did. The Old One had passed last winter, a season marked by death amid swirls of snow, ice and bitter, bitter cold.

She couldn't stay wolf always, and in her human shape Raven hated the cold. The bone-numbing chill was the one thing that tempted her to rejoin the human world. When she became wolf, she felt warm enough. Human was another story. No matter how many layers of stolen clothes she wore, she couldn't banish the cold from her skin.

After last winter, she'd nearly packed it in and given up. Only her pack of wild wolves had kept her in the cave, shivering when she was human, gritting her teeth and counting the hours until she could become wolf once more.

When spring had finally arrived, the pack had rejoiced. In summer and fall, every day had been a celebration of life, of living.

Until now. This day, winter started again. Early.

Shivering, she cursed her human form, hating the weakness of her olfactory senses, so sharp when she was wolf. Yet even as human, she sensed something was wrong, something more than the icy wind blowing over the mountains, more than the promise of snow in the air.

Beside her, Shadow whimpered.

"You sense it, too." Absently, she stroked the thick pelt of the wolf at her side. Her pack knew her scent, whether human or like them, and one or two stayed with her always. As protection and for company.

Two more heavy-coated wolves glided closer. The animals had started growing their winter coats weeks ago, their internal clock telling them the time had come. As human, Raven had noted the change and stepped up her gathering and storing, remembering the long winter the prior year. This year she'd vowed none of her pack would starve.

Despite her preparations, she still felt unsettled. Something was definitely not right.

Later, she'd change to her wolf-self and scout out the area, but now she needed to gather more wood. She thought she'd beefed up her food rations—nuts, berries, whatever she could find— enough. Years ago, in her human time, she'd learned to cure meat, but now she had no way to obtain the salt to make the brine. Yet her pack, always generous with their kills, had not protested when she'd taken choice cuts of meat to try and freeze them, burying them in the crevice areas where her cave dipped deep into the earth.

She wanted to be ready. Yet she worried that despite her hurried preparations, winter had

arrived too quickly. She needed human supplies—salt and matches, blankets and a newer
thermal sleeping bag to replace the tattered one
she'd stolen. A fire would be essential if she
wanted to survive the subzero temperatures this
high in the mountains. Even her pack liked the
warmth, though she needed it. Unlike her furry
pack, she couldn't keep her wolf-form with its
thick pelt indefinitely. Eventually, she went back
to the form she'd been born in, which pained her.

In the summer, when the hikers and campers
flooded the mountain, she'd taken what she
could, trying her best not to inconvenience
anyone. But now, with the icy north wind howling
over the mountains, humans no longer came to
the mountain. There'd be no choice for it—she'd
have to make a quick trip down into civilization
to steal what she needed, fast. As soon as the
storm passed, she'd do so.

A movement on the horizon caught her attention. The animal beside her growled low in her
throat. The other wolves moved up to flank her,
circling her with their silent protection.

Raven stared—uncertain whether what she
saw was real. If not a vision, she had a problem.
Despite the blizzard, a human climbed the

mountain, heading directly toward them. The furious wind and blowing snow had carried away his scent and he'd gotten way too close to her pack's sanctuary.

Of course, he might be lost. A lost human and a blizzard usually equaled death, unless she led him to safety. She preferred to do the latter. Two winters ago another man had died on her mountain. The search teams had nearly found her cave and her pack before locating his body.

With the human here, she'd be better off as wolf.

She dropped low to the ground and stripped off her clothes. Then, muttering her usual prayer, began the change from human to wolf. Over time, she'd learned to shape-shift in seconds. Now she'd track the stranger and find out what he wanted on her mountain in the midst of a blizzard.

Two of her pack flanked her, Shadow and Myst. The instant they stepped from the cave, snow and ice coated their fur, helping them blend into the wintry landscape.

Here, the human with his bright blue parka should stand out like a wolf in the city. But she and her pack could find no sign of him. The intruder had vanished into the storm.

Lifting her head, she scented the air. Nothing

but snow and ice and cold. She knew sniffing the snow would be equally futile. Either the man had fallen into a snow-filled crevice or he had taken shelter somewhere. Most likely the former, which wouldn't be good for her pack.

No choice but to find him. Raven hadn't survived seven winters on her own by taking chances. The man had to be close. No one, not even wolves, moved fast in a blizzard like this. Though the wind and blowing snow would have erased his tracks, she moved slowly and cautiously as she neared the area where she'd last spotted him.

With her keen sense of smell deadened, she had to rely on only her sight. If the man had been wolf, he'd have hunkered down under a tree, curled into a tight ball and let the snow cover him, making a nice pocket of warmth.

But he'd been only human.

There—she inched closer. She spied a bright yellow tent partially covered in snow. His own way of creating a pocket of warmth.

Making a wide circle, she checked the perimeter. Downwind of her cave with the view obstructed by a long line of trees. Satisfied, she put her head down and made her way back home. As usual, she'd remain in her wolf-form as long as possible, until her body betrayed her and forced her to return to her human shape. She much preferred being wolf. No reasoning, no fears, nothing but sensation. Easier, more exhilarating. And a hell of a lot warmer.

Inside the cave, her pack waited. The stranger's intrusion had caused the wolves to become agitated. As soon as she entered and shook off the snow, they surrounded her. Making guttural sounds and low whines, which she wished were actually a language, they communicated their unease.

Warmed by them, she let them huddle close until the frost that rimmed her fur melted. Then, slipping among the others, she touched noses, sidling wet fur against them and letting them sniff her, knowing her enforced calm and authority would eventually push away their anxiety. She was Alpha here, even though she wasn't wholly, completely wolf like them. Still, they always followed her lead. Today was no exception.

Outside, the storm continued to rage. The howl of the wind sounded ten times more chilling than any noise made by beast. Snowdrifts piled up at the entrance to the cave, blocking out the wind.

Gradually, the pack settled down and, as Raven had known they would, curled up in a huge pile around her and slept. She fell asleep as wolf, knowing she'd probably awaken as human, naked and freezing.

Despite the massive blizzard and near whiteout conditions, Simon knew his exact location. The GPS system he carried, along with the satellite link to base, ensured that. Yesterday, before the storm had started, he'd done a flyover. The sophisticated, heat-seeking instruments had revealed a possible human somewhere on this slope. Despite the weather warnings, he'd decided to go ahead with the search, knowing he could always change into his wolf form and hunker down under the snow.

But he wouldn't change unless he had to. This particular type of hunt was better done as a man. Until he knew the mental state of the person he hunted, he had to remain constantly on guard. As he had pointed out to Beck, too many careless Protectors had lost their lives to Ferals. Simon didn't intend to become another statistic.

He stopped, turning slowly to gain his bearings. To his left, he glimpsed the snow-covered valley he'd noted from the plane. That meant the Feral's lair would be to his right, higher up on the slope. He looked for caves, or tried to, but the shifting veil of snow made the search impossible.

For a moment he envied Beck on his mandatory vacation in the warm, sunny tropics. Beck had cursed Simon, but Simon knew his friend had been relieved.

Movement caught his eye. There, in the cluster of snowy firs. A wolf watched him, from no more than twenty feet away.

Cursing under his breath, he pretended to look away, never letting the animal out of his peripheral vision. The storm masked all scent, which meant he could be as much of a surprise to the beast as the beast was to him.

Still, he needed a better look to determine if the wolf was natural or the Feral shifter he'd been sent to find.

Dropping back, he took shelter from the wind inside his tent and began stripping off his clothing. Exposed human skin would lead to hypothermia and frostbite if he wasn't quick, so he began the change at the same time as he yanked off his shoes. Protectors were taught ways to facilitate the change and from a young age Simon could change to wolf and back in the blink of a human eye. He was grateful for this ability now, as still human, he shivered from the cold.

An instant later, he had his wolf's thick winter pelt as protection. Padding forward, he poked his shaggy head out from his makeshift shelter. He saw no sign of the other wolf.

He attempted to explore the area around his tent, but was unable to even locate tracks in the blowing, shifting snow. Searching in this kind of weather was pointless. Admitting temporary defeat, he returned to the tent and changed back to his human form. Crawling into his subzero sleeping bag, he zipped it closed and slept.

The next morning, Simon woke to the absolute stillness that always follows a blizzard. Snow had covered his small tent, weighing down the sides, yet insulating him from the wind and the worst of the cold. Warm and rested, he unzipped his sleeping bag and sat up, aware he'd have to dig his way out. He could only hope that when he emerged from the tent he didn't find himself surrounded by wolves.

First though, he had to make his report. Since his cell had satellite uplink, making connection would be no problem. The gadget worked in even the most remote places.

"Protector Simon reporting in." Simon kept his voice clipped, revealing nothing. The Council discouraged optimism when dealing with Ferals. More of a guilty-until-proven-innocent approach. "Feral spotted, location noted."

"How long before we have a full report?"

"I don't know." Simon clenched his teeth to keep from cursing. "There's a blizzard up here, making it difficult to properly assess."

"We need a time frame."

Inside the subzero tent, he was dry. Outside, the snowdrifts made him feel as if he were halfway up Mount Everest rather than the foothills west of Boulder. "Depends on how quickly I see her again. I've still got to make contact so I can do a better assessment. I'm thinking a month."

"Too long. Two weeks. Standard procedure when we're backlogged. Make another report in seven days." Before Simon could reply, the dispatcher disconnected the call.

Which meant Simon had been given two weeks to decide if the woman he'd spotted would live…or die.

Now he could curse, and he did. Stowing his phone in the backpack, he checked his watch. Eleven o'clock. Later than he'd realized.

Digging in his backpack, he located some field rations, popped the lid and scarfed them down. He had a choice—he could track as human, which would necessitate multiple layers of clothing in preparation for the frigid outside temperatures. Or he could hunt as wolf, with his warm winter coat and heightened senses.

For him, his no-brainer choice this time would be wolf. He had thick fur, calloused paw pads and his sharpened lupine senses. Even better, he'd perfected the ability to change back and forth from human to wolf nearly effortlessly. As long as he didn't stay wolf too long, the act of changing didn't deplete his strength.

Yesterday, the storm had rendered his nose virtually useless, but today the calm winds and unbroken surface snow would provide clues easily followed. Today, he'd hunt down the Feral and make an assessment.

He crawled to the center of the tent in preparation for his change. Time to resume the search.

Keeping her distance, Raven tracked the man, her jet-black fur standing out in the snow. As wolf, she kept low to the ground, uneasily skirting the tent he'd left up, which meant he planned to stay longer. She didn't understand why—the snowstorm had gone and the brilliant morning sunlight showed a clear path down the mountain.

So she followed him now, hoping to learn what he wanted with her mountain.

Her pack, hungry and wild, had wanted to hunt him as a trespasser. While part of her, the Feral, wolf part, understood and even agreed with this—the human half of her had known instinctively that to do such a thing would bring death and destruction upon their mountain. Plus, she was half human. She knew enough not to hunt her own kind.

Since she couldn't kill him, she'd watch him until he left. If he didn't go soon, she'd try to figure out a way to persuade him.

Ahead of her, where the man had ducked into his tent and lit some sort of lantern, his human silhouette showed he moved inside on all fours. Wolf Raven froze, every hair on her back raising. As she watched, the human shape undulated, flowed and changed. Became…wolf.

Stunned, Raven spun on her heels. Heart pounding, she bolted for her cave.

Once inside, she skidded to a halt, moving among her pack, sides heaving. Finally, letting their scent and their touch calm her, she went to her corner and crouched down on the cold stone. Changing back to human, she dressed quickly, gathering the Old One's heavy pelt around her shoulders.

She couldn't understand what she'd just witnessed. This man, this stranger with his unusual scent, had done as she did. He'd gone from human to beast, changing forms in the blink of an eye.

She hadn't known such a thing was possible in others. The entire foundation of her world had begun cracking under her. For her entire life, she'd believed she was an anomaly, a freak of nature. The only one.

Now, the appearance of this stranger proved she was not. The fact that she'd witnessed his change meant she was no longer alone.

She spoke the words out loud, once, twice and then again, savoring the sound. No longer alone. She should have felt exhilarated, energized. In a way, she did. Or, a tiny part of her did. Mostly though, she felt afraid.

She'd gotten used to a solitary existence. While she wouldn't call it comfortable—hell, who could say living in a cave was the cushy life—it felt safe. Untouchable. Loneliness wasn't something she often thought of, not with her pack always close. After all, the wolves were her own kind, too, and if the other side of her, the human side, went unfulfilled, too bad. She hated the human side anyway. All of the bad things that had ever happened had been when she was human. If she could have chosen, she would stay as wolf always.

But another like her, half wolf? The very possibility dazzled.

Again, she thought of the man changing into the wolf. Then she remembered the professor and the experiments he'd done to her, of the way he'd been intent on learning what gave her the ability to change shape from human to wolf and back again. She wondered if he had known there were others like her and, if so, why he hadn't told her. Or, when he'd decided she was no longer useful, why he hadn't taken her to them, rather than dumping her alone in the woods to die.

She had a clear choice. She could pretend she'd never seen the stranger change and delude herself that her world would always be exactly the same. Untouched, unchanged.

Or she could contact him, talk to him, make

him give her answers to the thousand questions now tumbling around in her head.

She sighed. She'd never belicved in lying—not to herself or to others—so she already knew what her choice would be.

She had to contact the stranger. But how? Did she want to meet him face-to-face? If so, as wolf or as human?

She decided she would sleep first, then make a decision.

Early the next morning, in the final hour before the sun rose, while shadows still overtook part of the mountain, Raven went to his tent. He'd already left. She could follow the human foot-prints he'd left in the snow, or...

Heart pounding, she took the liberty of entering the tent without an invitation.

Inside, she found little of interest. A warm, subzero-rated sleeping bag that she instantly coveted, a small, portable cookstove that ran on a metal can of compressed air and a backpack made of the same bright yellow material as the tent. His thick parka—another item she'd have liked to have ever since hers had been lost in a springtime flash flood—had also been left behind. From this she knew he'd gone hunting in his wolf-form. She approved of this, glad he hadn't brought shotguns or human weapons with which to kill his prey.

Panic fluttered in her throat. The small structure suddenly felt too warm. Confining. She didn't want to be trapped inside when he returned. As she'd intended, she left him a half-frozen rabbit haunch from last night's meal. Hopefully, he'd realize this was a peace offering and once he'd eaten, he'd take her up on her invitation to visit her cave. She'd make sure to leave an easy-to-follow trail.

Returning from his morning hunt as the sun rose over the eastern mountains, Simon stopped ten feet from his shelter. Fresh human tracks in the snow told him he'd had an early visitor.

The Feral. Suddenly wary, he approached the tent from the back side, circling around and then turning to check the perimeter.

The tent was now empty.

His snout told him she'd been there. As human.

Pushing through the flaps, he entered. She'd left a peace offering. Good.

Ignoring the rabbit haunch, he exited and followed her tracks to her lair.

He approved of the cave. Well hidden behind a clump of evergreens, the location provided protection from both the elements and any hapless humans.

Entering slowly, he stopped a few feet inside to let his eyes adjust to the darkness.

Back against one wall, the Feral watched him. She'd chosen to meet him as human. Unusual, especially in one rumored to be as Feral as she. At first, he narrowed his lupine eyes and, nose full of the musky scent of woman, stood motionless, waiting for her to make the first move.

"As man," she said, her low voice both husky and insistent. That voice sent a chill through him, a manifestation of something he immediately discounted.

"Change back to human," she repeated, as though unsure if he'd understood. "I want to talk to you."

Again the chill, the sense of foreboding. Ignoring this, he lowered his head and changed.

Man again, he climbed slowly to his feet and faced her. Even though they both were naked, for an instant he felt self-conscious doing so with his arousal jutting at her. But every shifter he knew became aroused when changing. Since she was of his kind, surely she knew this and would take no offense. He hoped.

But how Feral was she? How much did she know about her own kind?

Her eyes widened as she looked him over, her gaze sliding down the length of him. To his shock, he felt heat where her look touched him. A slow burn. Unable to help himself, he took a step toward her.

She made a sound, low in her throat. Not quite a keening, nor a wail, not even a whimper. He'd never heard the like before, whether in man or beast. Whatever it meant, the sound brought her pack to her, gliding into the cave silently, crouched low and ready to attack. To defend.

Shit. He'd forgotten about her wolves. Since his weapon was with his clothes, piled in a hasty heap inside his tent, if he wanted to survive, he had no other option but to change back to his animal shape.

Cursing his carelessness, he did. One second he was man, the next, wolf.

The clustered group of shaggy wolves froze. One whimpered low in her throat. Another—one of the males—growled. As a unit, they looked toward the woman for direction or command.

With shock, Simon realized she was their Alpha. This was unusual. Most Ferals adopted into a pack led the quiet life of a follower.

She made no sound, no gesture, nothing to indicate her next move. Instead, she stood and stared, her gaze locked on his, visibly shivering in her human skin. Then, without taking her gaze from his, her lips moved soundlessly as she changed, becoming wolf between one breath and the next.

Inwardly, Simon flinched. Not possible. The speed of her shape-shifting rivaled his, and he'd gone through years of training to be able to change so quickly. She was Feral, uneducated and alone. The speed of her change shouldn't be possible.

A low rumbling from one of the wolf pack made him push the question from his mind. Questions could come later, if he survived this first meeting.

The Feral-as-wolf took a step toward him. In her animal form, she was a hundred times more dangerous, all teeth and claws and thick winter coat.

Wolf-Simon stood absolutely still, prepared to fight if necessary, resigned to the fact that this would be one battle he'd be lucky to emerge from alive and unscarred.

For a moment the only sound in the cave was the steady thump of Simon's heart. Then, without even so much as a growl to warn him, the Feral wolf leaped, teeth bared.

Chapter 2

Raven didn't know why she thought she could threaten him with an attack. But she had wanted to intimidate him, so he'd tell her what she needed to know.

She thought it'd be easy, cut-and-dried. But she was used to being Alpha of her own natural-wolf pack. Perhaps part of her forgot he was also human and therefore subject to the powers of reason.

Therefore, though she weighed fifteen pounds less, when she launched herself, she half expected him to give way immediately. After all, her own wolves did.

He did not move.

She hit him hard, which should have rolled him, but he didn't go down. Instead, to her shock, he launched a counter attack, snarling and biting back, using teeth and jaws and claws that were easily twice the size of hers.

Locked together, they rolled on the cold stone, truly fighting. Her own pack formed a ring around them, watching from a respectful distance, their eyes glowing blue in the dim light. They would not defend her, not against another of their own kind. This fight for dominance was natural to them, their way. Whoever came out of this battle victorious would be their new pack leader.

Emotions—whether they *loved* Raven or not—didn't factor into things. They were wild beasts, nothing more, and if she humanized them, that was her own half-human fault.

None of that mattered. Right now, she had her life to defend. She was on top, her teeth inches from the other's throat, when inexplicably, her body began to betray her.

The change, unbidden, flickered through her. Not now! Not now! She'd surely die if she were to become human in the middle of this fight.

She hated this, hated that she could not control the impulses of her headstrong body. Oh, the second she became fully human, she could force herself into an instant change back to wolf, but the energy would drain her and render her unable to fight.

Damn it.

As the huge male wolf flipped her on her side, she felt herself becoming human. But she wasn't prepared to die.

The other—the wolf-man—hesitated. To her shock, though he could have easily ripped out her throat and ended this, he pulled back. His teeth merely grazed her skin.

As her wolves inched closer, ready to defend her since she was now human, the stranger glared down at her, his lupine eyes glowing.

She held herself perfectly still, waiting for him to decide her fate. His winning the battle on a technicality did not make him Alpha, at least as far as she was concerned.

With a flip of his head, he gave a mighty shudder, and became human, too.

"We need to talk," he said. His accent, the source of which she vaguely recognized, gave the words an exotic inflection.

Exotic! She snorted. What could be more exotic than two freaks who could change from human to beast and back again? She wanted to ask questions, to learn if his existence meant there were others, perhaps an entire pack of them, but fear held her back. Fear and an odd kind of stubbornness.

He held out his large paw—er, hand—as though he expected her to take it and let him help her up. To her own shock, she did.

Climbing to her feet, she let go as soon as she was standing, glaring at him, unsure what, if anything, she should say.

"Come." He led her to the corner of the cave where her discarded clothing lay in a heap. As he handed her the Old One's pelt, her nerveless fingers couldn't hold on and her coat slipped to the cave floor.

They both bent to retrieve the cloak at the same time, noses nearly colliding.

His nostrils flared. Though Raven jerked back, stupidly, she let herself get caught in his gaze. His eyes compelled her, drew her, with their irises so dark they were almost black. Beautiful, long-lashed eyes.

Belatedly, she jerked away. Even with her human nose, she could smell his desire. His engorged male part confirmed it. He smelled of mint and man and lust.

Raven remembered that scent. Knew it and hated it.

Horror filled her…and rage. Never again, she'd sworn once, and meant it.

Glaring at him, she bared her teeth, letting him see her fury and her fear.

Palms up, he dipped his chin. "I mean no harm. This usually happens with males when we change from wolf to man. Please. Get dressed."

While not liking the way he had her backed up against the wall, she wasted no time. Dressing in silence, she watched through her lashes as he stood naked in front of her, apparently impervious to the cold.

"You dress, too," she ordered.

"My clothes are in my tent."

Crossing her arms, she jerked her head toward the cave opening. "I'll wait."

He changed to wolf before she'd finished and padded away. When he returned, he was man again, and fully dressed.

In addition to his normal clothing, he wore a down-filled parka that she sorely envied, remembering the warmth of them from her days spent among other humans. She continued to watch him, wondering what he wanted with her mountain, her cave, her pack, her.

Finally he faced her. She lifted her chin, waiting. Now what?

"Call them off." He gestured at her wild pack, still circling them, uncertain and wary.

She didn't move. How dare he think he could give her orders?

His dark eyes narrowed. "Do you truly want this kind of trouble?"

Trouble. For the first time, she wondered if he had a weapon, a gun of some sort. If he had, then why hadn't he drawn it before now? Most likely he was unarmed. Still, she could not take the chance.

Her pack inched closer. Two or three of the more dominant ones snarled. A sharp thrill ran through her, followed by a sobering awareness of the potential danger.

She couldn't bear to see any of her wolves hurt because of her. Though she hated to give the appearance of obedience—she was Alpha here, after all—she spoke one word, using her sharpest, most commanding tone. "Back."

The wolves froze. She'd taught them a few

commands and they understood this one. Immediately, they fell back.

If the man was shocked, he didn't show it. Instead, he cocked his head and studied her through narrow eyes. "Will you talk to me?" he asked, his arrogant tone in stark contrast to his words.

This confused her briefly. Surely she hadn't grown so out of touch with the language of humankind that she'd misinterpreted him.

Meanwhile her pack watched to see what she would do.

She decided she wanted to hear what he would say.

"I'm listening." Her voice sounded rusty, no doubt from lack of use. "What do you want with me? Why are you here?"

"I came because of you." His gaze never left her face.

"Do you need help?"

Help? From him? For some reason, this made her uncomfortable, as though she'd donned the wrong human skin.

Odd thought. She filed it away for future examination.

"What do you mean, you came because of me? I am fine. I called no one, didn't ask for help."

"You're wild. You exist outside of the norm."

What a stupid thing to say. She let him hear the contempt in her voice. "So? Who cares what I do? I live my life as I see fit, as far from the humans as possible."

"You're human, too."

"Only part."

"Like me." He cocked his head, waiting. "Half and half."

There he had her, the entire reason she even let him come so close. Curiosity won over caution. "I hadn't known there were others."

"You thought you were—?"

"The only one. Alone."

A flash of pity crossed his face, making her grit her teeth. Finally, he nodded. "There are many more. Ordinary, like us both."

"Ordinary?" She couldn't hide her shock. "You think becoming wolf from human is ordinary?"

"Okay, wrong word." He flashed a casual grin, the impact of which she felt deep in her belly, making her hate him even more. "Regular people, like you and I."

Regular. People.

"I don't consider myself a person." Lashing out at him, partly because of the beauty of his smile, partly because something in what he said made her stomach churn, she all but snarled the words.

Her rage and fear hovered in the air, a solid thing.

At this, several of her pack inched closer, growling low in their throats.

"You can't deny what you are," he said, his voice calm.

"I am wolf more than human."

Again one of her wolves growled.

"No." Even though they could easily kill him, he didn't spare them a single glance. "You might want to be more wolf, but you're human, too. You're both. Human and wolf. You must learn how to live with both parts in harmony."

"Must?" She hated that he made her feel like a child, defending her right to believe as she wanted. "Says who? I don't need humans." She spat the word. "I have my wolves, my pack. That's enough for me."

His hard stare never softened. "I'm trying to give you a chance here. Work with me."

Since his cryptic words made no sense, she ignored them. "Go away."

He sighed. "All right, then. Why do you hate people?"

Hate people. Raven had never thought of her

loathing for the human race in such bitter terms, but maybe he was right. Since there was no way to put in words the horrors that she'd experienced at the hands of the human race, she didn't even try. "I avoid them."

"Semantics? Fine." He blew out a puff of air. "Why do you *avoid* people?"

"None of your business. Let's say I have my reasons, and leave it at that."

"You don't think I'll understand."

This time she allowed a slight smile. "You don't know what humans are capable of."

"There you're wrong. I do, believe me." His cold expression remained unchanged. "But not all of them are bad."

He took a step closer. Though instinct had her wanting to, she refused to retreat. Lifting her chin, she held her ground.

"What do you want with me? Why have you come here?"

"I'm a Protector." He said this as though he expected it to mean something to her.

"And?" she prompted, when he didn't elaborate.

He shook his head. He must have decided if she didn't know what Protector meant, she didn't need to. Instead, he continued to look at her. "I would like to stay and join your pack."

If he'd meant to shock her, he'd succeeded.

"Join my pack? Why?"

"To learn your lifestyle."

Riiight. This man wanted to learn her lifestyle about as much as she wanted to learn his.

Since, in her experience, people always lied, she wasn't surprised. But she *was* done, for now. She pointed to the cave entrance. "Leave."

Of course, he didn't move. Had she really expected him to?

Three of her wolves, again picking up the tone of her voice, glided closer, snarling low in their throats.

He barely glanced at them.

"You'd better do as I say. Leave."

"What will you do, set them on me?"

Raven opened her mouth, then closed it. Let him think what he wanted.

Flexing his fingers, he continued to watch her. "If I change, I can take all three of them."

"Maybe." Maybe he could. As wolf, he'd been the largest male wolf she'd ever seen, so she acknowledged the truth of his statement with a dip of her chin. "But can you take on my entire pack?"

As though her words had summoned them, the rest of her wolves surrounded them, ready to defend her if she signaled them to.

Though he had to realize the threat, he didn't appear worried. Even if he was good at pretending, the wolves would have scented his fear, as Raven would were she to change.

"Please," he said, the words sounded as though she'd yanked them from his raw and bleeding throat.

Though she knew they must have cost him, men like this one didn't like to ask for anything. Still she shook her head. "You need to go."

Instead of heading for the cave entrance, he took a step toward her.

Young, impatient and extremely bitchy in the aftermath of her first heat, the she-wolf Raven called Mandy (she didn't know why—some song she barely remembered from her horrific childhood), completely lost all self-control. She leaped for him, taking him down completely. Just like that, the rest of the pack was on him, snapping and snarling.

The man fought back, trying to change. But Mandy had planted herself in the middle of his chest and all of his attention was occupied with keeping her from reaching his jugular and ripping out his throat.

Watching, Raven knew she had to stop this now—if she could. She shouted at her pack to stop. One or two of the animals on the outer fringes moved back, but the rest of them ignored her. Raven felt the first flutter of panic in her chest.

"No," she yelled again. She couldn't let him die. His death would bring the eradication of her entire pack and their lifestyle. Nothing like the death of a human to bring out a thousand more, seeking revenge. They'd slaughter wolf after wolf after wolf, until nothing remained on this mountain but their bloody footprints.

"No," she screamed again, wading into the fray and yanking them away by the scruffs of their necks. After the first two or three, the rest of the wolves moved back. Even Mandy lifted her head, her muzzle red with his blood, though she did so with reluctance.

Raven ordered her to the back of the cave. Head down, Mandy slunk away, three other wolves flanking her. Raven made a mental note to watch her in the future. The time might come when the other she-wolf would want to challenge her for the role of Alpha.

Raven went to the man, meaning to help him. Still conscious, he waved her away and climbed slowly to his feet, bleeding from a deep bite in his arm and another on his shoulder. His dark eyes showed his fury, despite all the blood he'd lost.

"Thanks." One corner of his mouth lifted in what might have been either a snarl or an attempt at a wry smile. He held his mangled arm out toward her. "Do you have anything to wrap this? I need to stop the bleeding."

She grabbed several pieces of material from a bunch of old rags the pack used for a bed. "This is all I have." She'd always healed fast. Maybe he wasn't the same.

With a nod, he waited, his arm still outstretched, dripping blood. Crossing to him, she wrapped the clothes around him tightly, trying to stop the bleeding. But her fingers, unused to this sort of thing, were clumsy, and finally he took the rest of the clothes from her, binding his own wound. He waved away her attempt to help, even when he had difficulty tying the makeshift bandage with his blood-slicked fingers.

"Those are not very clean," she pointed out. "You run the risk of infection." Even though he didn't have a choice, she felt obliged to warn him.

"If I were you, I'd leave right now. If you head to the nearest town, you can find a doctor to help you."

Staring at her, he started to speak, but instead he swayed and crumpled to the ground without a sound. He must have lost more blood than he'd realized.

Great. Now she'd have to take care of him.

With a warning look at Mandy, she crossed to him and felt for a pulse. His heart still beat, and his chest still moved with his breathing, so he still lived. Since he was nearly twice her size, Raven knew she couldn't move him. Instead, she wrapped herself in her warmest fur pelt and headed out to his tent. She'd use what she found there to help keep the man alive.

Once inside the tent, she rummaged in his backpack and found a soft cotton T-shirt that would be easy to rip for a bandage. She also took his long underwear, jeans, sweatshirt, socks and snow boots. The sleeping bag she rolled up to bring into the cave. He would need that most of all. Without it, since her wolves would not pile together around him for warmth, the man would freeze.

All of this she carried back to the cave. Still unconscious and naked, the stranger had begun to shiver horribly from the cold. Beginning with the underwear, she dressed him as best she could, working the long johns up by lifting one leg then the other.

When she reached his man part, made small by the cold, she hesitated. Heart pounding, she tried to understand her fear. Part of her expected his eyes to snap open and the man part to lengthen and grow.

When nothing happened, she continued dressing him, next with jeans, then socks and shoes. The long-john shirt she put on him backward and left it unbuttoned, aware she couldn't lift his torso. The sweatshirt she couldn't manage so she abandoned that and placed it on the rocks beside him. Then, also backward, she put his warm parka on him, knowing the insulated coat would keep him warm.

Finally, she slid his feet into the sleeping bag and moved it up with steady jerks until she'd gone as far as she could (his waist). At least most of him would be warm and, if he woke enough to raise himself up, he could finish what she'd started.

Rising, she heaved a sigh. Unwanted guest taken care of, she went to her wolves to prepare for the cold night ahead.

Head throbbing, Simon's mouth felt so dry his tongue had melded to the back of his teeth. He opened his eyes slowly, squinting as the light brought pain. When he opened them more than a slit, everything swirled around him in a nonsensical kaleidoscope of color.

Where was he and what the hell had happened to him?

Heart thudding loudly in his chest, he concentrated on trying to remember.

When it all came back to him, he swallowed again, noting in confusion that he'd been dressed and covered with his heavy parka. He found that small human kindness promising. Ferals usually cared only for themselves. And because her exposure to shifters was nonexistent, she didn't know how quickly they healed. Already, his wounds were starting to close. Maybe he could use this to his advantage.

Pushing himself to his elbows, he looked around.

At the movement, the huge silver-coated wolf at his side let out a low growl of warning.

The Feral had given him a wolf guard? Without thinking, he curled his lip and returned the growl, though it sounded less menacing coming from a human throat.

The small sound was enough to bring *her* to his

side. The Feral. He watched her through slitted eyes, furious at his helplessness.

She looked savage, like a cavewoman from a long-ago era. Wearing the same badly skinned wolf pelt wrapped around her slender shoulders, shivering in her human shape, she knelt down by him. He noticed she chose a spot well beyond his reach. Pushing a battered tin cup toward him, water sloshing over the lip, she watched him warily, her stare unwavering, as did her wolf. Behind the two of them, he could see the blue-gray glow of other lupine eyes watching from the shadows, ready to attack.

He shuddered, tamping down his rage.

"That's water from melted snow." She nudged the cup forward. "Drink." Her words made puffs in the frigid air.

Water. He licked his cracked lips. He needed water as badly as he needed air. Hand shaking, he reached for the cup, wincing as pain shot through his shoulder at the movement. Somehow, he managed to raise the water to his mouth, sloshing some onto his hand. He lapped at it like a wolf, then slurped like a child, unable to raise the cup enough to tilt it and drink. Each swallow brought pain, and he wondered how he'd hurt his throat.

Her. The Feral. He shot her a quick glare. She was damn lucky he was a full-blooded shifter and healed fast.

In silence, she continued to watch him, her gaze alternating between his face and the cup he held loosely. Her eyes were blue, glowing softly even in the dim light.

Breathing deeply, he gathered his strength. Raising the cup again, he managed to take one sip, then another. This time, the icy water felt like heaven sliding down his burned throat. The cold even felt good on his teeth.

Grateful, he drank it all, then knocked the cup toward her with a clatter. "Thanks."

Taking it, she regarded him gravely, making him wonder how she'd look if she smiled. But then, most Ferals weren't human enough to use facial expressions—to smile or frown. He'd bet this one was. Already, she'd proven different than any other Feral he'd seen.

"If you can sit up long enough, you can fix your long johns and then put on your shirt." She pointed to his CU sweatshirt next to him. "You'll be warmer that way."

He made a mental note to put this in his report. Then, since the stone cave floor felt like ice on his back, he pushed himself up farther, using his elbows, teeth clenched to keep from swearing.

Grunting, he managed to pull the long johns off, turn them around and then he fumbled to try to button them. His vision blurred, making this difficult. Though he knew by tomorrow he'd be pain free and well on his way to healing, that knowledge did nothing to help him now.

Breathing hard, he rested for a moment, determined to complete the task. After he'd managed to button the bottom four, he quit, shooting her another look. Unmoving, she watched him with an unblinking stare that would have been disconcerting if he hadn't known what she was.

When he reached for the sweatshirt, again pain knifed through him, sharper this time. Sweat broke out on his forehead and trickled down his back, but he made no sound.

Somehow he managed to finish dressing. When he'd done so, he snuggled down into the sleeping bag, noticing how the Feral eyed his parka with undisguised longing.

He dipped his head toward her. "You can wear it."

To her credit, she didn't pretend not to know what he meant. Moving fast, she snatched the parka and retreated. Dropping her fur pelt, she kept her face averted as she slid her arms into his coat. The sleeves hung past her hands and the waist nearly to her knees.

Unaware of the comical picture she made, she zipped the front and raised the hood over her head. Then, returning her gaze to him, she crossed her arms.

If he'd expected her thanks, he was wrong. Of course, he'd expected nothing. Ferals weren't versed in the social niceties.

"You're welcome," he said, goading her.

Instead, she pointed toward the cave entrance. "As soon as you can walk, I want you to leave here. I've taken down your tent and packed everything for you." With a toss of her head, she indicated his bright yellow backpack.

Odd that she'd known the names of his articles of clothing—the long johns, sweatshirt and parka—as well as that she'd had enough knowledge to dismantle a tent and pack a backpack.

How Feral was this woman anyway?

This was what he'd come to find out. The less Feral, the more likely she'd be able to be rehabilitated. In order to make his report, he now had to convince her to let him stay long enough to

observe her. This was always one of the most difficult tasks of a Protector—gaining trust.

"Of course I'll leave as soon as I'm able. But
I'm not well enough yet."

Peering at him, she gave a hesitant nod, still
frowning. The sound of her wolves, snuffling
and moving around, was the only noise in the
cave.

Clearing his throat, he decided to engage her
in conversation. The scale he used to grade Ferals
had many variants, and the ability to engage in a
long conversation ranked highly.

"Do you live here?" He inclined his head,
meaning the cave. Though the background report
he'd been given indicated she did, her humanlike
actions and her well-informed manner of
speaking had him questioning the accuracy of his
information.

He'd never investigated a Feral like this one,
that was for sure. Most of them were little more
than half-made animals, unable to process even
the most rudimentary information in their ruined
brains. They'd have left him to die, ripped apart
by the wild wolves, and certainly wouldn't have
helped him after the attack.

Simon curled his lips into a smile. He liked a

puzzle, and the challenge this Feral presented had come along at exactly the right time in his career.

"Do you live here?" he repeated.

Pursing her lips, she didn't answer, so he tried again.

"I mean, if you have another place to live, how long have you been camping here?"

"None of your business. You seem well enough to go. So get up and take your stuff and head on down the mountain." Her tone was fierce, her expression completely closed off to him.

Since leaving wasn't an option, he simply closed his eyes, pretending his strength had suddenly deserted him. If she wasn't aware of the healing abilities of their kind, he didn't plan to enlighten her.

Then blinking up at her, he made a show of trying to keep his eyes open. "I'll leave as soon as I am strong enough to walk." He moved his arm again, this time wincing for effect. Already his pain had begun to lessen, though she didn't need to know that.

"Today," she repeated.

"There's no way I can hike down the mountain today." Though his playacting wasn't too far from reality, he knew he had to be careful not to overplay his part. The woman might be Feral, but intelligence glinted in her blue, blue eyes. No matter how wild she might be, he could tell she was far from stupid.

For what seemed a long time, she silently studied him, as though trying to make up her mind. Finally, she jerked her head in a nod. "You can stay one more night."

Her use of the word *more* caught his attention. "What do you mean? How long have I been unconscious?" More than a few hours would be extremely unusual for him.

Her clear gaze slid away. "One day, one night, and—" she glanced toward the cave entrance "—most of today. It's nearly sunset."

Simon swore, earning a sharp glare. His first report would be due in one day. He'd lost far too much time. Why, he had no idea. The altitude, maybe.

He'd have to ask for more time. Because of the immense backlog of cases, Ross hated when a Protector asked for an extension, but Simon didn't have a choice. His supervisor could hardly argue with injury and unconsciousness.

He just had to be careful to downplay what had happened. If Ross truly believed this Feral was a danger, he'd order Simon to kill her. Simon hoped like hell he wouldn't have to do that.

Despite what his friend Beck thought, while killing was often necessary, taking another life never felt good. Simon certainly didn't enjoy that aspect of his job. The only reason they called him Terminator was because when he knew killing was necessary, he didn't hesitate. Never had, never would. Not once.

The Feral woman made a sound to draw his attention. He refocused, surprised that he'd drifted off, but perfectly willing to use this to his advantage. Luckily, his little fugue appeared to be exactly what he needed. He didn't even have to continue arguing his case.

"One more night," she repeated grudgingly. "When we hunt tonight, I'll give you some of our meat."

He dipped his head in a silent thank-you, aware she'd understand that better than words. As courtesies went, by human standards her offer was small. But considering she was Feral and wild animals didn't share, this was huge. He made another mental note for his report, wishing he had his transmitter. He needed to check in soon.

If she'd packed as she said, then the transmitter was most likely in his backpack, beyond his reach. Though the signal would continually relay his location, until he punched the talk button and dialed in his code, he couldn't communicate with headquarters.

He still had one more day. Since he couldn't grab for his backpack without giving himself away, he'd get as much information as he could for his first report.

He cleared his throat. "Do you have a name?"

Her stare never wavered. "Why?"

He wondered if she believed that to give a name was to give power. He doubted it. Such a complicated belief would require a society of others. This woman was alone and, from the looks of things, had been for years, other than for her wild pack of animals.

Simon attempted a smile. "I wanted your name so I don't have to call you 'Hey, You.'"

"Don't." She practically snarled the word, her gaze spitting blue fire.

Taken aback, he cocked his head. "Don't what?"

"Smile. Don't smile."

Stranger and stranger. Knowing he had no choice but to go with the flow, he frowned. "Is this better?"

"Yes." She answered grudgingly. "Thank you."

"My name is Simon."

"Simon." She repeated his name under her breath. Then, as though having his name made giving hers easier, she lifted her chin. "I am Raven."

Another huge milestone. For the first time in a long time, Simon believed he just might have found a Feral who might be able to be rehabilitated.

Just then his transmitter, always on, buzzed loudly from his backpack.

Chapter 3

When the stranger's—*Simon,* she reminded herself—backpack buzzed discordantly, her entire pack went on instant alert. Stiffening, the wolves closest to her watched her for a cue on how to react.

Even Simon froze, wincing.

"My transmitter," he croaked. "Would you bring it to me?"

Transmitter. She vaguely knew the term, but for the life of her, she couldn't remember what it meant. Something not good for her or her pack, she thought.

Unsure, she didn't move. "Is this transmitter some kind of weapon?"

He frowned, and then slowly shook his head. "No. It's a communication device. If I don't talk to them soon, they'll send someone looking for me."

Though she heard his words, she couldn't read his expression, nor scent whether he spoke the truth. One of the things she hated about staying in her human form. "Them?"

"The people I work for."

She had no idea who they might be. Since the last thing she needed was to have this man call his job and give them his location, she made no move to retrieve his transmitter.

The thing buzzed again and his frown deepened as he realized she had no intention of retrieving it. He pushed himself up and made a weak attempt to lunge for his backpack. Easily, she slid it out of his reach and waited. If he was well enough to stand and make a move toward her, he was well enough to go.

Fervently, she hoped he was well enough to leave. Then she could go back to her normal life. His presence in her cave not only unsettled her pack, but reminded her of things from her past she'd rather forget.

But either his weakness was real, or something of her expectations must have shown in her face. Instead of pushing to his feet, he sagged back against the stone wall and sank to the ground. Crossing his arms, he glared at her, his expression darkening. "You really don't understand how important it is that I talk to them."

Since this was so patently true, she didn't bother to reply.

At her completely blank expression, he sighed. She watched as he made a visible attempt to relax. "Look, Raven, I'm serious. I only have a certain amount of time. There's a ticking clock. I have to report in."

Hearing her name spoken in his husky, deep voice sent a chill through her. Again, unsettling. "You aren't making sense. None of this matters to me."

"You might think none of this matters," he said. "But it does. If I don't check in, they really will send someone else. Another Protector, and he'll kill anything and anyone he believes threatens me. Including your wolves."

Though she took care not to show it, this statement alarmed her more than anything else he'd said. She would not endanger her pack. Her ragtag group of wild wolves trusted her to keep them safe.

"If that's true, you'll have to leave right away. You can take your transmitter with you."

Again his mouth twisted into that strangely attractive wry smile. "Yeah? How? I can't even sit up without help."

"Maybe I can rig some kind of sled." She put out the suggestion merely to see his reaction. In her past experience men, especially men like him, would find such an idea a challenge. He wouldn't know that she had neither the materials nor the strength to haul him down the mountain.

His dark gaze flicked over her, absurdly making her feel naked, which made her clench her teeth. "Rig a sled with what? And even if you managed to build something, how would you get me down?"

The way he echoed her thoughts made her wonder if he'd read her mind. Could such a thing be possible? She supposed so. If people could change into wolves, anything was possible.

She continued to stare at him. Despite her repugnance toward him, she'd never seen a human male so beautiful. The fact that he was like her, part wolf and part human, only made him more attractive. This infuriated her.

"Of course I could always push you off a cliff," she said softly.

"You wouldn't." He spoke with certainty.

This intrigued her. "How do you know?"

"You aren't stupid." He gave her a sharp look. "And I'm not, either." With that, he closed his eyes, effectively dismissing her.

Raven didn't move, not until the even sound of his breathing indicated he truly had fallen asleep.

While he slept, she took the opportunity to study him, closer than she'd ever dare while he was awake. Still wearing her human skin, she knelt down close to him and touched her nose to his hair, trying to decipher the complexities of his scent as if that could tell her why she felt the odd push-pull of him.

With her ordinary human nose, he only smelled like a man. So she couldn't understand why his scent made her want to touch her mouth to his skin and taste him. Not like food, no. She honestly thought if she could decipher the mystery of him and figure out his secret, she could vanquish the powerful longing that made her so furious and so restless.

But she couldn't and she wouldn't, so she rocked back on her heels. Another reason to want him gone.

Unsettled, she restrained herself from touching him again and pushed to her feet, more certain than ever that he had to go. In desperation, she even considered the feasibility of using his tent as a sort of travois and hitching him to her pack of wolves, harnessing their energy like sled dogs. A nice thought, but one she doubted they'd allow, even for her.

So it appeared she was stuck with him, at least until he regained his strength.

Heading to the other side of the cave, she took his backpack with her. She needed to take a look at this transmitter thing herself. If there was a way, she would disable it.

Pulling a small, black plastic box from the bag, she held it up to see better. A light on the side glowed softly red, indicating it was on. Though she lived in the wilderness, she made an occasional foray into town, staying at a hotel. This thing couldn't be that much different than a television remote control. Easily, she located the power button on top and pressed it, holding it until the light went off. There would be no calling or making reports until she'd gotten him out of her cave and off her mountain.

Oblivious, Simon continued to sleep. Careful

not to wake him, she moved quietly to the back of her cave and hid the backpack, tucking it into a stone alcove where a narrow shaft led farther into the earth.

Then, eager to use the free time before her unwelcome guest woke, she signaled to her wolves. Once they'd all moved near the entrance to the cave, she stripped off her clothes, muttered her invocation and changed into her wolf-self. With her wild pack at her side, she went out into the cold, white snow to hunt.

The icy, packed snow felt cold beneath her paws, rapidly numbing them. She shook herself, increasing her stride until she ran flat out, her wolves streaming at her side. She ran until her muscles ached, ran until she had to pant, ran until she thought she might have banished the disquiet the man called Simon had brought with him.

Then, she got down to business. Now she could hunt for that night's meal.

Ever conscious of time constraints, even as a wolf, she kept her hunting time short, killing a half-frozen rabbit and marking the spot with its blood so her other wolves knew where they could find the meat. They converged on it while the body still steamed. Snapping and snarling, they fought among themselves over the food. She knew this small morsel would scarcely dent their hunger, and that was her intent, to spur them into a thorough hunt for more game. When they'd eaten their fill, they'd return to the cave.

Moving away from them, she searched out another rabbit to bring to the cave so she could feed Simon. He'd need meat to regain his strength if he were to ever be well enough to leave.

Once she'd returned to the cave, she shook the snow from her fur and, as wolf, padded over to check on the human. Satisfied he still slept, she made the change back to woman and dressed, shivering as she did. A bitter chill had settled over the mountain and she knew the temperatures would plunge lower once the sun set.

Waiting while her pack finished hunting, she felt their absence keenly. She was their Alpha and as such should be leading their hunt, not remaining in the cave. But keeping watch over Simon was a necessity, too. She couldn't take the chance he'd notify others about her location.

Others. Her restlessness returned at the thought. She'd had no idea there were others. Others like her. Growing up she'd read books about werewolves, seen the horror flicks, knew the legends. But those stories were all fiction.

Werewolves didn't exist. Except for her. She believed she was an anomaly, a freak of nature. Until Simon had come to her mountain and she'd see him do what she'd thought she alone could— change into a wolf.

Because of this, a hunger burned inside her that had nothing to do with food. She hungered for knowledge, the desire to know more about her kind, her people. Yet she knew if she asked, he would tell her, and the serenity of her perfect world would be forever shattered.

Damn him.

One thing she'd never been, even when the professor had kept her caged like a wild animal, was a coward. Nor would she become one now. That night, while Simon was still too weak to move, she'd get the answers she so desperately wanted. And then, once she'd learned what she needed, she'd figure out a way to remove him from her life.

An hour later, her wolves returned with what was left of their catches. Game had been plentiful as the smaller animals emerged from their burrows in search of sustenance. Raven took her portion and a portion for Simon before burying the rest in the coldest part of the cave. This meat would serve as food the next time a snowstorm struck.

Though she couldn't communicate this to them, her pack trusted her and watched without protest while she carried the meat away. They were well fed and sated, having already feasted during the hunt.

When Simon began stirring, she used a few of her precious stash of matches and wood to make a small fire. Then she spitted the last two rabbits and hung them over the flames to let them cook until she judged them done.

In her world, doing such a thing was tantamount to a gift. Once the human intruder accepted, he'd have no choice but to answer her questions.

The scent of roasting meat must have done the trick to bring him fully awake. Moving better than he had earlier, he sat up, dragging his hand over the stubble on his rugged chin.

"Hey," he said softly, his deep voice again sending a chill down her spine.

Teeth clenched, she made no reply, gesturing instead to the meat slowly cooking, waiting with her breath held to see if he would accept her small offering.

"That looks far better than it should." A smile hovered around his well-shaped mouth. "I'm starving."

Damn the man and his smile. Hurriedly, she looked away, staring at the meat, which now appeared to be turning black on one side.

Turning her back to him, she retreated to her small fire pit. Yanking the rabbit from the flames, she carried a haunch over to Simon and dropped it near him.

"Eat," she ordered, retreating a safe distance away. Her own stomach growled. Usually, she ate her meat as wolf, raw right after the kill. Months had passed since she'd eaten cooked meat, and as she took the other rabbit for herself, tearing off a leg and biting into it, she resolved to cook more often.

He struggled to push himself up onto his elbows. Again she wondered how much of his weakness was real and how much was an act. Despite all his talk about time constraints, he didn't appear to be in any hurry to leave.

Once he'd managed to sit up, he snatched up her gift without hesitation and tore into the meat as if he hadn't eaten in days. The rabbit was tough and stringy, overcooked on one side and close to raw on the other, but he wolfed it down, making low-pitched sounds of gratification.

Watching him devour the food fascinated her, though for a different reason than her pack, who despite their full bellies nonetheless coveted his meat. Only respect for Raven, their Alpha, kept them from fighting him for his meal.

When he'd gnawed even the gristle from the absurdly tiny bones, he tossed them to the closest wolves, then licked his greasy fingers clean. Despite the sudden lump in her throat, she continued to eat her own food. Then, mimicking his actions, she rose, bones in hand. She handed all of the bones to only one wolf, the smallest of her pack, a runt wolf she called Ben. The others watched silently, though they knew better than to try and take his bounty from him. As long as Raven stood guard, none of her wolves would dare to steal from Ben.

Only when Ben had swallowed every morsel did Raven return her attention to Simon. "You've been fed. Are you strong enough yet to leave now?"

He ignored this, so she rose and went to add more wood to the fire. When she turned, he still watched her, his dark gaze intent. Knowing.

She hated for a man to look at her like that.

"Come here," he ordered. "You have questions, don't you?"

Questions. Despite her brave intentions, having him know what she'd been thinking made the words stick in her throat.

Unwilling to let him see how uncomfortable he'd made her, she went and sat, well out of his reach, affecting an insolent air, dropping her bottom on the cold cave floor with a thud.

It took everything she had to keep from wincing.

Clearing her throat, she tried to sound as though she didn't much care. "Questions? Maybe a few. I didn't realize there were others like me, until I saw you. Of course, I only learned what I could do, what I could become, completely by accident."

His sympathetic gaze made her hate him. "No one taught you?"

Though her cheeks heated, she kept her anger in check, knowing it was irrational. "No. I don't think they knew themselves. Have you always known what you were?"

He nodded. "You know nothing of our people's history, then, of how we came to be?"

"No. How could I? I've always been alone."

"Always?" He frowned. "What about your parents? I don't understand. They had to know. Why didn't they teach you?"

"Both my parents died in a car accident when I was small. I barely remember them. Child Protective Services searched, but they couldn't find any relatives. I went to live in one of their homes. Human homes," she emphasized.

Again, he smiled. She felt the power of that smile like a punch in the stomach.

Pretending not to notice, she held herself absolutely motionless, staring into the distance at nothing.

With a sigh, Simon's smile faded. "Are you ever happy?"

"Of course I'm happy. Why?"

"Are you always so serious?"

"Do you always answer a question with another?"

"No." Again that flash of a smile and the clenching of her gut. "Sorry. You're right. I like you, Raven. Let me tell you a bit of our history."

She didn't want him to like her. But she did want to hear what he had to say, so she nodded.

"This is an abridged version of pack history."

"Pack?" Startled, she emphasized the word. "Like my wolves?"

"Yes. And like our kind. Centuries ago, when humans roamed the earth in tribes, our kind roamed the earth in packs. Our histories suggest we were some kind of freak mutation, if one takes the stance that all mankind evolved from apes. If not, then we were divinely created. Just like with pure humans, there are two schools of thought. Both are hotly debated. Many believe we shifters were created in glory, specifically made by the finger of God."

Despite her completely nonsuperstitious nature, Raven shivered. For so long she'd considered herself closer to a spawn of hell, one of the names the professor had called her; hearing her natural abilities described as heavenly felt akin to blasphemy. She snorted. She wasn't entirely sure she even believed in the existence of God.

"Either way," he continued. "Our people have been around as long as pure humans."

This made little sense. "Then why haven't skeletons been found? Or tombs? Archaeologists would have announced such a thing, and the world of humans would know and accept us."

She continued to watch him closely, wanting to

know the instant he began lying to her. She knew he would, sooner or later. Humans lied. They all did. Why should this one be any different?

"You really don't know anything, do you?" Before she could retort, he continued. "When we die, no matter what form we're in at the time of death, our bodies revert back to human. And, besides old age, if you're a pure shifter, there are only two ways to kill us—fire or silver."

One word stuck in her mind. "What do you mean pure? How can you be anything else?"

He flashed yet another quick, beautiful smile. "Humans and shifters have been known to interbreed. Someone with even one-fourth of shifter blood can still change. We call anyone who is part human a Halfling."

"Halfling." The word sounded almost foreign on her tongue. "How do you know which you are?"

His gaze sharpened. "Who were your parents?"

Somehow she managed a careless shrug. "No idea. All I know of them are from vague memories. Like I said, they died when I was five. I barely remember them. I don't even know their names."

"We can find out." Unknowingly, he dangled

her most secret desire in front of her like a T-bone steak. Or maybe he did know, with the mind-reading thing and all. "Our kind keep detailed records. Your birth is sure to be recorded somewhere."

Despite this, her heart continued beating, steady and sure in her chest. Concentrating on breathing normally, she frowned. "I wouldn't even know where to begin to look. Or how."

"Anything you can remember will help. The pack is very organized. We've organized ourselves into Councils at local, state and national levels, all operating under the humans' radar."

Despite her best efforts, she couldn't contain her shock. "National? How many of you—us— *are* there?" All the time he'd been talking, she'd pictured a few thousand, no more.

One corner of his mouth curled and she could tell he was trying hard not to smile. She silently thanked him for that. "Hundreds of thousands. Maybe millions. Since we don't list shifters as an ethnicity on the U.S. census, we don't really know. And that's in this country alone. There are more overseas, in every country on the map."

Hundreds of thousands. Millions. She didn't know whether to laugh or to cry. While she sat stunned, trying to digest his words, the next thing he said was like an arrow straight through her heart.

"You might have family somewhere, you know."

Her heart fluttered in her chest. She stared. "Family?"

"Yes. Your parents surely had brothers or sisters, parents of their own. You might have grandparents and a whole slew of aunts and uncles and cousins, ready to welcome you with open arms."

Damn this man. How dare he dangle in front of her like a carrot her secret dream, her most heartfelt desire? She could scarcely breathe, so heady did she find the notion. She'd never dared to think, to hope, that there might be anyone out there who cared whether she lived or died.

Yet even now, part of her, the wild, aloof, lupine half, scoffed at the idea. Preposterous.

She had her wolf pack. Why should she need anything more? Besides that, if she truly had family, why had no one ever rescued her from the hellhole of her past?

"I doubt that," she told him slowly. "No one has ever tried to find me."

"Maybe they don't know about you."

A second passed while she considered. During her years of captivity with the professor, he'd often gloated that no one was looking for her.

So either they didn't know about her or she had no family. She couldn't let this stranger know how much she had hoped and dreamed for the former to be true.

Stupid, stupid girl. This was part of the reason she preferred to be wolf. The only time she could entirely erase these foolish longings was when she was in her animal state.

Time to change the subject. She still had more questions.

"I try to stay wolf all the time," she told him, ready for different types of answers. Still, it was hard to choose what to ask when she had so many questions swirling around inside her head. "But my body won't let me. Worse, I have little control over it. After a few days tops, my body keeps changing back. Why is this?"

"Because you're primarily human."

"I don't want to be!"

Ignoring her outburst, he continued doggedly, as though reciting from a textbook. "You were born human and when you die, your body will die as a human. Look at it this way—" he waved away her protest before she could voice it "—the wolf part of you is a bonus."

"Why do you say it like that?"

Now he focused on her, bringing the full weight of his dark gaze to meet hers. "Like what?"

"As though you're telling me something you've memorized, something you must state exactly the same way you were told." She took a deep breath. "Something you don't entirely believe in."

"Believe? That's not even a choice. I'm telling you facts, nothing more, nothing less. That's all I have to go on. You might want to stay wolf longer, but wanting won't make it so."

Sullenly, she crossed her arms. "Too bad. Life is easier as wolf."

A weird expression crossed his face, a look of shock, of recognition, as though he himself had thought the same thing. "The ones who try to stay wolf too long go mad."

"What about the ones who try to stay human?" She had no idea if anyone ever did such a thing, but it only seemed fair.

"Same deal. There are numerous documented cases of shifters who refuse to change. They also go insane."

"What happens to them?"

Apparently the open, sharing part of the conversation had abruptly ended. He shut down. There was no other way to describe it. As though her last response had flicked some sort of internal switch.

"How long are you able to keep your wolf shape?" he asked, his tone neutral.

"Why? Do you think I'm crazy?"

After a startled moment, he laughed. "No. But I myself have tried to push the limit. I can remain in my wolf shape for six days."

"And that didn't make them label you a nutcase, worthy of being shot or carted off or whatever the all-powerful pack does with their mentally unstable?"

He laughed. "No. What about you? How long?"

"I've stayed wolf a few times for three days."

"That's pretty good."

"Really? When I do that, I'm wiped out. How do you manage six? When I try to stay wolf longer, my body revolts and changes back."

"I don't know," he said slowly. "I just can. When I was younger, we trained to try and remain wolf longer."

"And when it's over? What happens then?

After six days, is the shift back to human violent?"

"Not really. Just involuntary."

"Like mine."

"Yes." Again he studied her, considering. "You seem to have a pretty clear understanding of your nature for someone like you."

"Like me?"

"You know." He waved his hand. "Wild. Unschooled."

Clenching her teeth, she had to work not to show anger. "I live like this by choice, not because of mental illness or drugs or anything like that. I lived around people for most of my life, until recently. And just because I wasn't raised by my natural family doesn't mean I'm stupid."

"Ah, yes, I forgot. I apologize." He sounded unrepentant.

She shrugged. "I had little formal schooling, but I've always read a lot. I guess you could say I'm self-educated. I've been on my own a long time."

A moment passed. Then Simon cocked his head. "I've read your file," he said softly. "I know about the professor and what he did to you."

Chapter 4

If he'd claimed he could fly, he couldn't have shocked her more. "You know…what?"

"Everything."

She winced. She couldn't help it. "Then you know he lives in North Boulder and works at CU, right? That he's a highly respected man?"

"Yes." The way he watched her told her there was something more, something he wasn't telling her.

She didn't care. She shot him a defiant look. "Are you aware if he learns that I'm still alive, he'll send someone to kill me? Did you know that?"

"I told you, the organization I work for is thorough. We know what he did to you."

"No. You can't." She closed her eyes, hating the shame washing over her, but powerless to deflect it.

"I'm afraid so. I know about the cage, the experiments. The videos."

Rage filled her, a fury so deep and powerful her entire body vibrated with anger. "If you know all this, then why hasn't he been arrested?" She clenched her fists, her inner wolf snarling and snapping. "So help me, if you tell me what he's doing is not against the law, I'll kill you."

"Because he's dead."

Just like that, her antagonism evaporated. "What? Dead? When? How?"

"The police think he was murdered." Again, the way he watched her made her uncomfortable.

Then she realized why. "Ah, so you think I killed him, don't you?"

"Did you?"

"No." She clenched her hands into fists, deciding to tell him the truth. "But I would have if I could. I despised that man."

"That's understandable after what he did to you."

"Tell me how he died."

They stared each other down. She could hear the snow melting outside in the absolute silence.

Finally, he nodded. "He was killed at his laboratory. Someone broke in. That's how we learned about you. When the police searched the lab, they found a hidden room, a large cage. There were journals chronicling your time there."

"Of course." She shuddered. "He was a vile, filthy bastard."

"How long?" he asked softly. "How long did he keep you?"

Old habit made her want to hang her head with shame, as though *she'd* done something wrong. But she hadn't and she wouldn't, so instead she lifted her chin and held on to his gaze like a drowning swimmer holds on to a raft. "Three years."

He swore, that deep voice of his so low and fierce it sounded like a growl. Several of her pack raised their heads and watched them more closely.

"How did you survive?"

She shrugged, pushing back a stab of anger. A question like that didn't really deserve an answer, but she answered anyway. "I just did. You learn to do what you have to in order to live."

"You escaped?"

"No. He freed me. Actually, he planned to kill me, but at the last minute couldn't do it. Instead, he dumped me high up in the mountains, above the tree line. It was the middle of winter and he didn't leave me a coat."

"You should have died of exposure."

"I know." She remembered that long afternoon and night vividly. Of course, she would—that nightmare still haunted her dreams. "If I'd stayed human, I would have. But I changed. As wolf, I knew enough to move down the mountain into the trees. I found a sturdy evergreen to shield me from the wind, and burrowed myself a nest below the snow. I stayed there until the first blizzard had passed."

He nodded, his expression bleak.

Even speaking about it made her shiver. During that first week, she hadn't thought she'd ever be warm again. But she'd survived, she'd lived and become stronger. That was the important part.

"How?" he asked, making her realize she'd spoken out loud. "How did you survive?"

She gestured at her wolves. "Them. They found me. Apparently I'd stumbled onto their hunting grounds."

Studying her pack, who watched them with intelligent eyes, he swallowed. She found the small movement of his throat inexplicably fascinating.

When his gaze returned to her, the bleak anger had vanished. Either that, or he'd pushed the rage deep inside him, as she did. "You're Alpha. Did you have to fight them?"

"Of course. And yes, I was wounded, and yes, I fought more than one. But I won and I healed and I became part of their pack. Their leader. They trust me and I trust them. I've been here ever since."

"Six years."

"Yes. But I still don't feel entirely free of him."

"The professor?"

"Yes."

"Back to him." He took a deep breath. "There's more. After you, there was another."

Stunned, she stared. "You mean he…?"

"Another little girl."

All the horrible things he'd done to her… Raven closed her eyes against the pain. "How little?" she whispered.

"Younger than you. Maybe ten or eleven then."

Her stomach churned. "What happened to her?"

When he didn't answer, she turned on him,

letting him see her agony. "What happened to her?" she repeated, wiping at the tears spilling like a silver stream down her cheeks.

"We don't know. We think she escaped."

Turning her back to him, she let herself cry. She wept for the poor child—or children—after her, and prayed they hadn't had to endure the same horrors she had. She suspected they had. Caught up in her torment, her chest felt like it would burst.

Then he touched her. Turned her and drew her into his chest. "Please. Don't cry. He's dead. He can't hurt you or her ever again."

Such a simple human kindness from a stranger could have been her undoing, she who'd been without touch or compassion for so very long. Instead, him holding her somehow gave her strength, enabled her to pull back from the black abyss of her past.

"Thanks," she mumbled, moving away. Then, as realization dawned on her, she rounded on him. "You're standing. You can get up. You can walk."

He nodded, his intent gaze never leaving her face. "Yes, barely. But I am regaining my strength. I should be able to get out of your way by tomorrow."

She debated making him leave right then, but night had fallen and there was no moon. "Thank you for telling me about the professor. Because of that, I'll let you stay."

"If I leave now, they'll only send another."

"Why? I've lived up here for a long time. My pack and I keep to ourselves. Why do you people think you need to bother me?"

Now he looked away. "When we learned about the professor, we learned about you. There are more like me, searching for the other girl. When they find her, she will be evaluated, just like you."

"Evaluated how?"

"I make a report."

"Then what happens?"

"That depends on what I say in my report."

"I'm extremely uncomfortable having you judge me that way."

"I'm good at my job. The Society knows I'll tell them the truth."

"The Society?"

"The organization I work for. The full name is Society of Protectors."

She nodded, pretending she understood. Though she found the name reminiscent of a college fraternity, she thought the group itself might be much more dangerous.

"So if I get you the transmitter, you'll call in and make the report. What will you tell them about me?"

He stared, his mouth a hard line in his rugged face. She stared right back.

When he didn't answer, she decided to give him the words she wanted him to say. "You could tell them I deserve to be left alone."

His mouth twisted. "I could, but they wouldn't listen."

"I thought you said they'd know you told the truth."

"It's too early. They know I wouldn't make a full assessment so soon. Also, I'd never tell them a Feral deserves to be left alone."

"But that's what I want," she cried. Taking a deep breath, she spoke again, and willed her voice to sound calmer. "What about what I want? Don't they take that into account?"

"No. As far as they're concerned, there are two choices with Ferals."

"Ferals?" Another new word. "What do you mean?"

"Ferals are shifters that live outside the norm."

"Like me."

"Like you," he confirmed. "And there are two kinds of Ferals. Those that can be rehabilitated and those that cannot."

She didn't like the sound of this. "Rehabilitated? Explain."

"Assimilated into society."

Something in his voice… Outraged, she glared at him. "You mean trained? Like a pet dog?"

"Not at all," he began, but enraged, she wouldn't let him finish.

"Okay, I get that part. But what about the others, the ones who cannot be rehabilitated? What happens to them?"

When he looked at her, his eyes were flat and cold, his mouth once again a hard line. "We have to kill them. They're exterminated."

The instant he said the words, Simon knew he'd made a mistake. Though he'd only told her the truth, she wasn't anywhere near ready to hear it.

She recoiled, her wide sapphire eyes turning frosty. "Exterminated? Just because someone doesn't fit into your precious society, you kill them?"

Put like that, it did sound rather heartless. He

thought back to his conversation with his friend and fellow Protector Beck and grimaced.

"Most of them are dangerous," he said softly. "I've seen several go mad and attack humans and other shifters."

"How can you lump so many individuals into a group? Surely you have to look at them one by one."

"That's what I do. Investigate the Ferals and assess them. I rarely meet one who isn't a menace to himself or others."

She snorted, her eyes flashing blue fire. "Humans are dangerous, too. Look at the terrorists. But they don't have organizations to go around and kill them."

"Terrorists?" Her statement intrigued him. "How do you know about terrorists?"

"I can read," she scoffed. "I try to keep up with current events. Once or twice a year, I hike down into Boulder for supplies. I pick up the papers, magazines, whatever I want."

This surprised him. The more she talked, the less Feral she appeared. "Really."

"Really. Don't you think I'd get bored, living up here with nothing to do but hunt, eat and sleep?"

"Where do you get the money?"

"I have no money." She lifted her chin, her look daring him to chastise her. "I steal when I have to. I've gotten pretty good at Dumpster diving, too. And a lot of time, people have more than they need, so I borrow the extra."

"You know, that is what brought you to our attention. Some people reported the thefts."

"Maybe." She shrugged. "I did what I had to."

He decided to ask something else that he'd wondered about. She was beautiful, clean and, he grudgingly admitted, sexy as hell. A complete contrast to every other Feral he'd ever investigated. "What about hygiene? Baths, brushing your teeth and such?"

She laughed. "Do I smell?"

Swallowing, he shook his head. In her human form, she had a scent like flowers or meadow grass. And woman.

"I'm not a complete savage." Climbing to her feet, she went to the back of the cave and returned with a large plastic storage tub. "I keep a regular supply of soap, toothpaste, shampoo and all that in here."

He wondered about her monthly flow, but decided not to ask. No doubt she had feminine hygiene products, as well.

"This is more like an extended camping trip than some savage, half-wild existence, isn't it?"

Her smile grew wider, making him want to smile back. But he remembered how she seemed to hate his smile, so he kept his face expressionless.

"To you, maybe. But I have to fight to survive. I chose this life. Maybe I should give you your transmitter. You can make your report, tell them I'm civil and clean and not a danger to anyone. I'm already...rehabilitated." She stumbled over the word, grimaced, and then continued. "Once you tell them that, they—you—can leave me alone."

They'd never let him do that. He'd tried to tell her, but apparently she wasn't ready to listen. They'd never leave her entirely alone. Not until they were one hundred percent certain she wasn't insane. Not until she'd proved she could live a normal life.

One of the things he hated about being a Protector was their absolute, unshakable tenet that their way was the only right way. *Live Our Way or Die* should have been their motto rather than *Protect and Defend*.

His thought shocked him. Until that very second, he'd never allowed himself to even think a single criticism of the Society. When had he become so cynical? His thoughts sounded more like the sentiments espoused by Beck. The same bitter sentiments that had made Simon realize his friend was due for a long, calming holiday.

Apparently, so was Simon. Maybe he needed a break worse than he'd realized. Witness his slower than usual healing time. When he returned back to base, he'd make sure and schedule one, preferably someplace tropical and warm. A few weeks there and he should return to normal.

Normal was good. After all, his occupation was his life. He could no more separate *Simon* from *Protector* than he could stop breathing. What he did for a living was right and necessary, he knew this deep within his heart.

The Society of Protectors had existed for centuries. Their methods, though not universally agreed upon, worked. Shifters were safe, their existence secret from most humans. The pack society functioned well on so many levels, enabling them to retain all their history and unique qualities, while appearing to blend with humankind.

If their laws seemed a little harsh, who was he to question what worked? The laws of nature were no less savage.

Clearing his throat, he forced his attention back to the present. Normally, he wasn't one for esoteric mental rambling.

The Feral, Raven, still watched him. He wondered if she would really give him his transmitter. He'd actually gotten strong enough to retrieve it himself, but he needed to keep the appearance of helplessness long enough to finish his evaluation of her. If he wrestled with her over his transmitter, she'd know he was well enough to leave.

The prospect of wrestling with her held far more appeal than it should have. Furious at his lack of self-control, Simon banished the image from his mind. Mating with a Feral was the ultimate taboo. Even considering such a thing made Simon feel dirty, unclean.

He wouldn't allow such thoughts ever again. He had a job to do. One thing he'd always prided himself on was the quality of his work. He did his job well. He could wait a little longer before making his report.

Over the years, he'd investigated hundreds of Ferals. He'd brought some, quite a few, actually, back into society, guiding them through rehabilitation with a firm hand. Others, he'd had no choice but to exterminate. Some, like the rabid

Feral who'd gone so mad he killed anything that came near him, had been easy decisions.

This assignment was different, true. Raven was nothing like any Feral he'd ever seen. Not only was she beautiful, but intelligent and not the slightest bit savage.

Assessment. What he'd seen so far seemed extremely promising. She appeared less and less Feral the more she talked. Easily rehabilitated, if only he could get her to agree to at least *consider* giving society another try.

Blinking, he realized he'd drifted off again. The transmitter. They'd been discussing the transmitter. "Will you give me my transmitter?"

"I don't know." She swallowed, the movement of her long throat graceful. "Honestly, I'm afraid."

"Of my report? I've already told you I can't make a full assessment so quickly. What I tell them now will be taken into consideration, but the final report is what matters."

"What would you say?" She dragged her hand through her hair. "I really *am* already rehabilitated."

"You'd have to prove you could live among humans."

"I can." She lifted her chin. "I have. I simply choose not to."

"Maybe you need a vacation," he suggested gently. "Go into town for an extended stay."

She narrowed her eyes. "Why would I want to do that?"

Careful. "For proof. Documentation. It might be good for you, you know. Soften some edges, break up the routine. Give the humans another shot." He gestured around the cold, bleak cave. "Imagine getting to sleep on a soft bed, to take long, hot showers."

Unfortunately, as he spoke, he got a mental image of her naked, standing under the showerhead, water running over her full breasts and down her taut, flat stomach. His body responded, going instantly hard. Shit.

What the hell was wrong with him? When had he become so depraved?

Though she had to be unaware of his arousal, her nostrils flared as though she scented it. "I like my life the way it is," she repeated stubbornly. "I won't pretend to be something I'm not."

Speaking of scent, he could almost swear he could smell the musky scent of female desire. It had to be a trick his own mind played on him, wishful thinking. Had to be, but still his traitorous body, already engorged, thickened.

Hellhounds. Lurching toward his sleeping bag, he kept his back to her as he climbed back inside. "Tired," he muttered for effect, pulling the down-filled bag up around him and trying to focus. Job. Task. At. Hand. Rehabilitation. Then a nice, long vacation for him. Some place far, far away. No mountains, no snow, no cold.

No Raven.

"I don't want to live in town," she repeated. "No, thank you."

"Just think about it," he urged, sounding as though he'd swallowed broken glass. "Not as a permanent thing, just as a short break. You already said you periodically go down into Boulder. So why not try staying a few weeks or a month?"

"You don't understand." Her breathless tone only succeeded in exciting him further. "I don't *want* to be domesticated. I like my life exactly the way it is."

"Domesticated?" Latching onto the word, knowing he had to focus or risk drowning, he forced out a laugh. "You make it sound as though I'm asking you to become someone's lapdog."

Lapdog. Bad choice of words. He instantly pictured her doing a sexy lap dance on top of him.

For hound's sake, this nonsense had to stop.

Completely unaware, she stared at him. Was it a trick of the light, or had her pupils become larger, darker?

"What else would you call it? I'd have to stay in human shape. Living in human society, you have to abide by their rules. I couldn't become a wolf whenever I wanted to."

Trying like hell to picture the last Feral he'd worked with, a wrinkled middle-aged woman with yellowed, chipped teeth and rolls of fat, he nearly missed what Raven was saying.

"You're worried you wouldn't be able to change?"

"That's exactly what I meant." She gestured with her graceful, long-fingered hands when she got excited.

"Of course you can change," he scoffed. "We all do. We just have to make sure no humans see."

"But I don't have to worry about that now. Here in the mountains, I'm free. I can go where I want, do what I want, with no one watching over me. If I want to be wolf, I become wolf. No rules, no boundaries."

Simon felt a stab of envy, which he quickly squashed. "That's not entirely true. Rules exist in nature, just as they do in society. You have rules. You said yourself you were careful to avoid hurting humans."

"Common sense. Kill or hurt something that's higher up in the food chain, and all the others come looking for you."

She leaned close, bringing him a whiff of her scent, feminine and alluring. Why the hell had he touched her to begin with? He knew better than that.

But he'd only been trying to offer comfort, not bring on this inappropriate desire. Damn. He'd just about wrestled his damn arousal to the ground. Now, it surged back, twice as strong.

He forced himself to concentrate on his end of the conversation. "Even in a wolf pack, one has to learn to consider others. You might be Alpha, but you still have to look out for the rest of them."

She shook her head, sending her long, tangled hair flying. "By choice, not because someone makes me. True, I'm Alpha. They defer to me and in exchange, I look out for them. I'm happy here and I won't abandon them. Make your report and then leave me alone."

His regret was genuine. "I can't."

Raven cursed, surprising him. "I don't understand. I'm not bothering anyone."

"You've stolen from campers a lot over the years. There've been many reports, so many that you risk having your wild pack hunted."

"That's against the law!"

"Is it?" He raised a brow. "You know, this is the first time I've ever had a Feral argue with me."

"Don't call me that!" The ferocity in her voice lashed at him.

"What? Don't call you what?"

"*Feral.* I'm beginning to hate that word. I'm not Feral, not at all. I'm just me. Raven."

Reaching for him, she gripped his arm. "Tell me honestly that you wouldn't rather have my life. Look me in the eye and tell me that. Maybe then, I'll believe you."

Simon stared. Far too busy trying to calm the raging inferno of his desire for her to answer, he shook his head. He both wanted her to let him go and to come closer.

She came closer, until her nose touched his. He bit back a groan. He wanted to kiss those full, parted lips. He knew she'd taste sweet, like wild berries fresh from the vine.

This had to stop. If he let himself do even one of the things he imagined doing with her, he'd turn himself in immediately. Expulsion from the

Society, court-martial, all of these would be in his future then. And he'd deserve them.

Him. Simon the Terminator. What the hell was wrong with him? Maybe something had happened when he fell. He certainly had knocked all the sense from his head. Hopefully after he got a good night's sleep, he'd return to normal.

He had to.

When he didn't answer, she flashed him a triumphant smile. "Your life sucks," she said with much satisfaction. "No, thanks. I'll pass."

Sucks. Another evocative word. Hellhounds. He pushed the thought away. "You have no idea what my life is like."

"I do," she insisted. "You forget, I've lived in society, among them. I've tried it. Didn't like it. I've got everything I need and I much prefer this."

"You were in a cage," he pointed out. "Not exactly normal living."

"Before that. Growing up. I never fit in anywhere. Here, finally, I do."

To his relief she leaned back, away from him, and gestured at her small cave. "This, and my wolves, is much better than the cruelty of humans."

Cruelty. The professor. Blindly, he grabbed on

to the one thing that might be able to keep him from yanking her on top of him and ravaging her mouth.

He swore under his breath.

"What?" she asked, eyes wide and impossibly blue.

Again he felt that jolt of lust. There had to be another reason. Maybe the need to make a report had him unsettled. That had to be why his reactions were so off. Though he didn't understand how he'd become such a slave to rules and routine, his inner clock, something he'd always been vaguely aware of, insisted he contact the Society and do it now.

Yet the Feral—the woman—*Raven*—had his transmitter and showed no sign of wanting to return it. She didn't know that if too much time passed between contacts, they'd send someone looking for him. Another Protector would come and, believing Simon's life to be in danger, he'd be authorized to kill the Feral on sight.

To kill Raven.

He glanced at her again, trying to decide how to explain the situation to someone who'd have no idea what he meant. Again, her beauty startled him, again the powerful attraction rocked him to the core.

"I need to report in," he rasped.

As if preordained, the transmitter let off a shriek. Simon jumped, as did Raven. She turned and stared at the back of the cave, which must be where she'd stashed his backpack.

"I thought I turned the damn thing off," she said.

"Not possible."

"I see that."

The transmitter shrieked again.

"What does that mean? Low batteries?"

"No." Expression grim, he pointed. "That's the alert signal. I haven't reported in and it's been forty-eight hours. If I don't respond within ten minutes, they'll send someone else."

Chapter 5

"But seriously, I turned it off."

"I told you, you can't. Even if you switch the power to Off, there's an internal battery that keeps the homing device working."

Now she cursed.

"Let me have it." Then, seeing her furious expression, he softened his order with a "Please."

"Against my better judgment," she retorted, rising and stomping to the back of the cave. She retrieved the backpack, digging out the yellow electronic device before stowing the pack away.

He caught it neatly. "Thanks."

Sat silent while he flipped the switch on, turned the dial and punched in some numbers.

He shot her a glance while he waited for whoever to answer, but she stuck her chin out.

"I don't care. I'm not moving. I want to hear what you have to say."

"Fine." He kept his tone clipped. Finally, someone answered. "Caldwell reporting in. I got the alert signal. Yes, all is clear."

The dispatcher then put him through to Ross. Simon told his boss about his injury, though he omitted the crucial fact that a wild wolf had bitten him. Without actually lying, he made it sound as though he'd had some sort of skiing mishap.

Ross voiced professional concern. "Are you all right?"

"Yes, I'm better now." Simon knew he sounded confident and authoritative. "Ready to make my second report."

Unable to resist a glance at Raven, he saw she was grinning. He knew she thought he would now tell them she wasn't a menace to society so they'd leave her alone. She didn't understand. The Society didn't work that way. Until Simon made a complete report, they would consider her a dangerous Feral.

He'd been given two weeks. He'd need to use all of it.

"Yes, I've made contact." He swallowed. "She's much less Feral than I expected." He went on to tell them she was more or less "camping" in the cave, about her cleanliness and civility. All good things.

"Good, great, fantastic." Ross's falsely pleasant tone alerted him. "But I'm afraid it's too late."

Alarm bells went off. "What do you mean?"

"We know what happened. The transmitter picked up the attack and we're aware you're injured and need help. Don't worry, you don't have to say anything. We know the situation."

"There is no situation." Simon scratched his head. "Seriously. I've already healed and the wolf that attacked me was wild, not the Feral woman."

"Right." Total sarcasm. "Just sit tight. We'll get you out."

Stunned, Simon could barely keep his tone civil. "Listen to me. I'm not in any danger. You don't need to send anyone. Let me finish here and—"

"Too late. A chopper is already en route with your replacement. We'll bring you home in that."

"No need," Simon repeated, his heart beginning to pound. "Call them back."

"He'll be there shortly. And don't worry," Ross continued on as if Simon hadn't spoken. "Once we get you patched up, we're sending you on vacation. None of this little aberration will go on your record."

On his record? Aberration? What the hell?

"What's going on, Ross? This is not like you."

"End of conversation." Then, while Simon was still sputtering, Ross hung up.

Stunned, Simon stared at the transmitter, unsure what to think.

"Thank you." Raven grinned at him. "That should have done it. Now they'll leave me alone, right?"

"No." Heart heavy, he grimaced. "They've already sent someone else." His mind whirled. In his entire career, he'd never left a job unfinished. Nor would he now. It was a matter of personal pride with him.

This Protector would kill Raven on sight. No questions asked. None were necessary, because Ross believed she'd attacked Simon.

"Why?" Raven came closer. "You made your report."

"They don't believe me." He knew he sounded bleak. "The transmitter picked up your wolf attacking me. The locater beacon is so precise, they knew I was immobile here, in your cave. They think you're keeping me prisoner."

She watched him, arms crossed. "This is bad," she said slowly. "Really, really, really bad, isn't it?"

"Yeah." He took a deep breath, wondering if she could sense his inner thoughts like he sometimes sensed hers.

Raven nodded. She didn't gasp or wail or rail. Instead, she lowered her head and took a deep breath. "How long do I have before he arrives?"

Done with pretending illness, he pushed to his feet. "I don't know. He's already en route. We've got to get out of here now."

"We?" Her direct stare challenged him. "I don't recall inviting you to join my pack."

"I know how they think. I can help you."

"Why would you want to do that?"

He took another deep breath. "Because this is my fault. This new guy has been given immediate orders to kill you."

She stared at him with those impossibly blue eyes.

"Do you understand? He's being sent here to kill you."

"They're crazy," Raven sputtered. "Murderers.

How can you condone something like that?" Before she'd even finished speaking, she began gathering her meager belongings, tossing them into a bright red backpack she pulled out of somewhere.

Words caught in his throat. A kill order, because of his mistake. Worse, Ross had refused to listen to reason.

Granted, headquarters was only following standard procedure. Knowing that didn't make things better. Raven's life was in danger because of him.

He felt betrayed. He'd been given orders to sit tight and relax. Help was on the way.

Direct orders. Someone else would now take over this case. Even that phrase bothered him. Raven was not merely a case. No way would he let her die. Not in this lifetime. Though Simon had no idea when this replacement Protector had left, what his ETA might be or what kind of fire-power he'd be packing, he damn sure didn't plan on sticking around to find out.

He was going to save this Feral's—Raven's—life. She didn't deserve to die. And, hellhounds be damned, he'd make his report and finish up with this job.

Raven made a sound of frustration, drawing his

attention. "What do I need to do?" Though her voice sounded steady, panic shone in her eyes.

Once again, the words stuck in Simon's throat. His new plan, necessary as it might be, went against everything he believed in.

But everything he'd believed in had changed. Though a kill order had been given, in all fairness, Ross had believed it was justified. The Society didn't operate like that. They all took the same oath, to be fair and impartial, to assess and report.

Until now.

So he'd do what he had to do. Go on the run with his case. His rehabilitation-ready Feral. And continue to do his job until headquarters could be made to pay attention. He'd observe, watch and make notes, file his reports and, after a two-week time period, make his assessment. He wouldn't harm her or her pack unless one of them made a move to hurt him.

Like her she-wolf had done when she'd attacked Simon.

Not Raven's fault.

Simon shook his head. Now knowing her name, he didn't like that he thought of her with such familiarity. His job was to remain objective, dispassionate. To observe and assess, not fraternize or sympathize.

His job. His entire life. He always put everything into his assignments. His dedication was unparalleled.

"Simon?" Raven repeated. "Help me out here. What do I need to do? Give me some thoughts, or even a direction. Obviously, I have to leave my home. I'm not ready to die."

"I'll help you," he heard himself say. "Come on," he grabbed her arm. "We've got to get out of here."

Behind them, one of the wild wolves growled. Jerking her arm free, Raven quieted the beast with a look.

"Don't touch me." Turning from him, she continued to cram her things into her pack. She didn't comment on his miraculous recovery. Maybe she'd already suspected he was exaggerating his symptoms.

Though if so, why wasn't she furious instead of… What? He studied her. Compassionate? Nonchalant? Or simply desperate?

A mystery. Another puzzle piece to try to fit into place. He filed this info away for further speculation.

"We don't have time for this." Maybe finally

the urgency in his voice got to her. Or quite possibly she had finished. Either way, she yanked the zipper closed and slipped her arms in the frayed shoulder straps. The backpack appeared to be ancient, on the verge of tearing at the seams, ripping wide open and spilling its contents on the ground.

She raised a brow. "Time for what?"

"You know." He gestured toward the cave entrance, meaning the unseen threat on its way. "You asked for my help, for direction. I'll give it now. If you want to live, you'll need to do as I say."

Her amazing eyes narrowed. "I don't think—"

"Then don't." Rudely interrupting her, Simon crossed his arms. "Where'd you put the rest of my stuff?"

She made no move to retrieve it. "I still feel I should go alone. These are your people, not mine. You stay and intercept them. I know these mountains. My wolves and I will be fine. I don't need your help."

Barely suppressing a snarl, he shrugged. "This isn't up for discussion. You might be Alpha to them," he indicated the waiting wolves, "but not to me. I'm going with you. Would you please point me in the direction of my things?"

A second or two passed while they stared at each other. He couldn't help but wonder if she meant to fight him, the way the wild wolves did, to prove she was his Alpha. If so, they both knew she'd lose.

Finally, she crossed the cave and reached into one of the wall crevices. Pulling out his backpack, she handed it to him, her face expressionless.

"Are you ready?" he asked again.

"I am." She sounded surly, but Simon didn't care. His entire focus was getting as far away from this place as possible before his replacement arrived.

"Let's move out." He started for the cave entrance.

"Wait."

"What?" Trying to keep the impatience from his voice, he stopped and turned.

"I know you want to go, but I'm sorry. I travel alone with my pack. It's been nice to meet you." She sounded awkward, as if the polite human phrase felt foreign to her. "Good luck with your job and everything. And thanks for warning me about the other that's coming. Take care."

He nearly gaped at her as he realized she was saying farewell. "I've already told you that we don't have time for this crap."

She narrowed her eyes. "You're not going with me. I don't trust you."

Ah, now her actions made more sense. In the world of wolves, if another wolf could be beneficial to the pack, he was never turned away.

"Watch." Simon removed the transmitter from his bag and slammed it to the rock floor. Then, to make sure it shattered, he stomped his heavy hiking boot over the broken shards of plastic, grinding it into the stone. He'd use his cell phone to check in. The last thing he needed was a homing beacon tracking his every move. "Better?"

Slowly, she nodded. "Fine. You can go."

Even as she spoke, she moved toward him. He didn't flatter himself, but he suspected she didn't want to lose contact with the only other person like herself that she'd ever met.

"We'll go as far as we can before dark, then we'll stash the packs and our clothing. After that, we'll travel as wolves. It's more difficult for their infrared heat sensors to track us when we're animals. The instruments can't tell natural wolves from shifters."

She stared at him, hard and considering. "You know I can only keep my wolf shape for three days. Is that going to be long enough?"

"I hope so." He answered honestly.

"If not, I'll try to hold my shape longer." She frowned. He could see her thinking, could almost read her mind. When she spoke again, she confirmed it.

"Why are you doing this?" she asked. "We barely know each other."

"It's my job," he said simply.

"Not if you go against them."

She was right, in a way. But things were a thousand times more complicated. How to explain the tug of connection he felt with her? He couldn't and therefore, wouldn't.

"Look, Raven. This is my fault. I can't walk away and let him hunt you down. I know how these people operate. You stand a better chance with me. I owe you that."

For the space of several heartbeats she stood utterly still, staring. He couldn't read her thoughts this time, nor did her clear, blue eyes give him any hint.

Finally, she dipped her chin. "You owe me nothing. Let's go."

Simon didn't see whatever signal she gave her pack, but the wolves circled them, moving with them. Two ranged ahead and several stayed behind. The rest flanked both sides, near enough to see, but not to touch.

Nostalgia came out of nowhere, blindsiding him. In his early training for the Society, the trainers had often taken several children into the woods to change and hunt as a group. There, they'd learned pack rules, both human and lupine. The experience had been one of the bright spots of an otherwise bleak childhood.

They traveled past the place where he'd pitched his tent, down the side of her mountain and up another. As they crossed the next ravine, keeping to the path that Raven claimed to have traveled many times, they heard the sound of an approaching chopper.

"Hellhounds," Simon cursed "They really wanted him here fast. We've got to hide."

Simultaneously, they dove for the nearest copse of evergreens to take cover. The pack of wolves melted into the shadows of the forest.

Raven blew air from her nose.

Side by side, crouched low to the snow, even in his human form, Simon swore he could catch a hint of her tantalizing scent.

His body stirred, even in the midst of danger. Adrenaline had always felt like an aphrodisiac to him. To distract himself, he eyed the copter. "They didn't even bother to have him approach with stealth."

Raven shook her head. "Why should they? They already told you he was coming."

"True." Mood growing blacker by the second, he watched the chopper approach and considered. "I guess they never guessed their star Protector would rebel."

"Is that what you're doing, rebelling?" She made it sound like a ten-year-old boy running away from home.

"I don't know." Because he'd already lied enough, all he wanted to give her now was honesty. "Yes. When the Society gives an order, we're supposed to follow it."

"Are you really the star Protector?"

He gave a terse nod. "Was. Won't be after this."

The roar of the chopper grew louder. It hovered over the valley below her cave.

"Do you think they'll try to land?"

He shrugged. "Maybe. More likely they'll get low enough for my replacement to jump out." He pulled a pair of binoculars from his pack. "I want to see who it is."

"Be careful he doesn't see you. That bright blue parka of yours isn't exactly camouflage."

He acknowledged her comment with a wry grin. "Which is another reason we'll soon be changing to wolves."

As the helicopter lowered itself, they both squinted into the sun, trying to see. From the distance, all they could see was the chopper, blades whirring, kicking up snow.

"There." Raven pointed. "Someone jumped. He's wearing red. It's almost as loud as your blue parka. Boy, you guys sure favor brightly colored snow wear."

Putting the binoculars to his eyes, he adjusted them, grunting as the red shape came into sharp focus. Bundled up the way he was, Simon couldn't make out any details about his replacement other than the face, and that he didn't recognize. The man—boy, really—looked young and eager. He must be new to actual fieldwork. Those were often the most hard-assed—they hadn't had time to become jaded or to question.

"I don't know him." He put the binoculars away. "Let's keep moving until we find a safe spot to change."

With a shiver, she nodded. "I'll be glad to become wolf. It'll be much warmer."

Again, they moved out. Her wild wolf pack materialized and ran with them again, several running crisscross over their tracks. Simon wondered if she'd somehow communicated an order to them, asking them to help cover the escape.

As soon as the thought occurred, he scoffed. Wild wolves didn't talk, nor could humans speak to them. Any actions by them that were beneficial were merely the result of coincidence, nothing more.

Moving carefully in the deep snow, they trudged over two more hills, through a snow-filled valley, then started up another mountain. Though the clear sky and bright sun made for a picturesque day, the icy wind whipped around them, sending snow to sting their faces. As they climbed, the bitter chill in the air hurt their lungs when they breathed. Ahead, they could see the end of the tree line as the snow crunched under their feet.

"We'd better change soon," she pointed out. "If not, we'll be running out of options until we go over this pass."

She was right.

"There." He pointed. "That last group of aspens. I know it's not much as cover goes, but it'll be easy to find again later. We'll pack our belongings under those rocks and change there."

"Okay." Quickening her stride, she headed for the grove of tall, narrow, white trees.

Way behind them, they heard the roar of the chopper. They both turned to watch as it gained altitude before disappearing into the bright blue sky.

Simon's replacement was on the ground. He wondered if the new Protector had started to climb the slope to her old cave. Once there, realizing it was deserted, it wouldn't take him long to find their tracks. Even though the pack of wolves did a good job obliterating them, they were animals and couldn't completely hide the shape of human boot prints. Plus, Raven was well-known to travel with a pack of wolves. Either way, they would be easy to track.

They didn't have much time.

As soon as they reached the aspens, Raven began shedding her clothes. Moving more slowly, trying not to watch her, he began doing the same.

With one final glance at him, her lips moved as she muttered to herself and then she changed.

Human, he couldn't help but watch, once again fascinated by the swiftness of her transformation. When she stood before him completely wolf, her thick pelt was the inky color of a moonless night, shining with health.

If wolves could laugh, she appeared to be laughing at him. Hellhounds.

Naked, shivering in the bitter cold, he grabbed her clothes and bundled them into his pack along with his own. He stashed the pack between several large boulders, tucking the coats underneath.

Then, taking a deep breath, he began his transformation.

The wild wolves watched from a distance. One of them whined, but for the most part they seemed to take such a miracle in stride. Of course, though they were brethren, they could neither reason nor wonder.

Change done, as wolf, Simon again looked at Raven, though now he primarily "saw" her with his nose. Yet even with his wolf eyes, he found her beautiful.

Tossing her head, she took off running.

Without hesitation, Simon followed, the wild wolves close on his heels.

Days blended into nights as they roamed the mountain. They moved as pack, hunted as pack and slept as pack. The difference between the wild wolves and the shape-shifters faded as time went on, and Simon felt he could remain wolf forever. Now he understood Raven's words, and finally, after years of hunting them, sympathized with the Ferals who refused to return to human form.

He knew if he could have kept his wolf persona indefinitely without going mad, he would.

On the morning of the third day, another blizzard hit.

They had plenty of warning—the sky turned the color of slate and the wind contained the moist scent of snow.

The first snowflakes were dainty and sparing, then the snow began falling in earnest and soon a heavy curtain of white impaired visibility. People died in whiteouts like this, and wild animals instinctively knew to take shelter.

If Simon and Raven could have communicated better than a few whines, grunts or barks, they would have discussed the need to find shelter. As things went, a swift glance at each other and then at the sky was more than enough.

With the pack still trailing behind them, they headed farther down the mountain, looking for a cave, an abandoned miner's shelter, anywhere they could take refuge from the snow.

Luckily, they came across a locked hunting cabin. Wolf-Raven and Wolf-Simon alternated throwing themselves against the wooden door until the frozen lock finally gave.

Once the entire pack had filed inside, she changed to human and bolted the door.

"There's a fireplace," she told Wolf-Simon. "But no wood in here. If there's a pile outside, we'll never find it in this storm. But I'm going to look."

He nodded to show he understood. At that, she muttered a few words under her breath and changed back to wolf. Padding toward the door, she nudged it with her head and disappeared into the blizzard.

The wild wolves settled themselves on the floor. For wild animals, they seemed unusually unperturbed at being confined inside. They trusted Raven that much.

Raven had her own problems to deal with. She knew that night the temperatures would dip well below freezing. The cabin would provide some shelter, but if they had no fire it would still be unbearably cold. Even as wolf, she'd already felt the cold, already shivered. She didn't know how much longer she could fight off her body's desire to return to human shape. She knew she'd reached the limit of her ability to remain in her lupine shape. With every breath, her body constantly tugged and pulled at her, attempting to change.

Though fighting this took the remainder of her diminishing strength, still she fought. If she allowed her body to become human, she knew she would die. No way her furless human skin could survive in these temperatures. So she fought to keep control and remain wolf, though if she made it through this night she would have surpassed her previous limit.

She returned to the cabin, a large stick in her mouth. Dropping it near the fireplace, she barked twice to let Simon know she'd found wood, then headed out into the storm to retrieve more. An instant later, Simon followed. Though the task would be a thousand times easier as humans, they had no clothing. Naked, they wouldn't last a minute in the subzero temperatures.

She'd help all she could, especially if that

meant they'd have a small fire to keep them semiwarm through the night.

But her internal battle took its toll on her energy. She lost count after the fifth or sixth trip. They'd carried in all the smaller pieces of wood, and the larger logs remaining would take more work.

Hating her weakness, Raven watched as Wolf-Simon clawed at the woodpile, leaping back as several logs tumbled down. One thumped him solidly in the shoulder and he yelped.

Concerned, Raven started forward, but Simon merely shook himself, sending snow flying from his fur, and bared his teeth at her, warning her to back off.

Several good-size logs were now on the snowy ground. These Simon could not carry in his mouth, so he began pushing one toward the door, using his paws and nose.

Taking a deep breath of icy air, Raven did the same. Finally, they managed to assemble a small collection of logs on the floor near the hearth.

Raven changed back to human and bolted the door closed.

"These logs are pretty wet," she said, more to herself than to him. "Somewhere around here, there's got to be lighter fluid and matches, or something. Maybe if I can get a fire going, the logs will burn."

She found some old newspapers in a cupboard. "Look. And there's lighter fluid and a lighter."

Somehow, despite her shivering, she managed to get a small fire going. The damp wood smoked and sputtered, but it burned.

Close to the hearth, huddled together in a pile, the exhausted wolves curled against each other, forming a protective cocoon against the cold.

Still wolf, Simon waited for Raven. Once she'd changed back to wolf, she curled into his side.

As her body temperature cooled, she slipped into sleep with her snout buried in Simon's damp fur, his scent strong and familiar and oddly reassuring.

Halfway through the night, while the storm's fury beat against the log walls, Raven's body changed as she slept. She became human.

Raven woke, aware something was very, very wrong. Mouth dry, heart pounding, she opened her eyes to utter darkness and the scent of wet fur. She felt a flash of panic until she remembered where she was. With the pack of wolves, safe inside the tiny cabin.

Except once again, her body had betrayed her.

She could try to change back, but from past experience knew the attempt would fail and only sap her strength.

Shivering, she wrapped her arms around her middle. The small fire wasn't enough to warm her. The temperature in the room was below zero. She needed to build up the fire.

Edging away from the still sleeping pack, the cold hit her. Without fur to protect her, her skin afforded no protection whatsoever. Her shivers became violent, body shaking, teeth slamming, shudders. She grabbed a tattered blanket off the bed and wrapped herself in it. Moving close to the fireplace, she pushed another damp log into the smoldering pile, praying the fire would blaze. Yet all that accomplished was to make smoke. The minimal warmth barely changed the temperature.

Still, she huddled close, wishing she had Simon's thermal long johns and his parka. Hell, right now she'd give her right arm for his down sleeping bag.

Meanwhile, the pack of exhausted wolves still slept. Simon slumbered in the middle of them, his glossy gray coat rising and falling with his breathing.

She added another log to the fire. More

smoke, fire hissing, stuttering, trying to go out. Cold, so cold.

Gradually, her shivering subsided. Not a good sign. If she couldn't regain her wolf shape, she'd freeze to death. Unless the collective warmth of her wolves could get her warm. Praying, she crawled over to them and attempted to burrow into Simon's furry side.

Chapter 6

Violent shivering roused Simon from a deep slumber. Slowly, he opened his eyes, resisting the urge to explore with only his nose, knowing those olfactory senses were too frozen to work properly.

The dim glow from the pitiful fire allowed him to see somewhat. Raven's wild wolves surrounded him, curled on all sides. They slept a kind of hibernated sleep, lowering their body temperatures as far as they could and still survive.

The shivering didn't appear to have disturbed them. Only him. Half human, he hadn't been able to succeed in reaching unconsciousness as thoroughly as they.

Raven.

He saw no sign of her. Alarmed, he stuck out his muzzle, seeking her scent. His nose encountered…human skin instead of fur. Hers.

Shivering, furless Raven. Somehow, she'd changed in the night while they slept.

Eyes half-open, he saw she was semiconscious. She shivered in huge, violent, body-shaking tremors. Again, Simon touched his nose to her. Her skin felt cold, clammy. The small fire had burned to merely embers and what little warmth it could provide was not enough to heat the cabin. Even now, wind whistled through the leaky walls, around the corners, battering the solitary window.

He could see her breathing, her breath freezing the moment it left her lungs.

Outside, the cold and the howling wind made the air temperature well below freezing. In the cabin, the walls were able to blunt some of the wind's force, but he'd still bet it was in the twenties, if not the teens. No way a naked human could survive in temperatures like this, even with her wolves piled around her for warmth.

If she didn't change back, she'd die. One look

at her terror-filled eyes and he saw she knew this already. Had she tried?

Since as wolf he couldn't communicate, Simon forced his own body into a rapid change back to human.

Instantly, the cold hit him. Damn. Reaching for Raven, he wrapped his naked body around her, trying to warm her chilly skin with his rapidly cooling but still-warmer flesh. He told himself he could ignore his fierce arousal—normal after a change, the cold would take care of that easily.

They fit together like a hand in a glove.

"Raven," he called. No response. Lightly shaking her, alarmed at the way her head lolled lifelessly, he repeated her name. "Raven."

Her eyes fluttered open, then closed. Her shallow breathing and irregular pulse told Simon that she hovered on the verge of unconsciousness. If she went to sleep now, most likely she'd never awaken.

He couldn't let that happen. He hadn't come this far, defied so much, to simply let her die of the cold.

Again he spoke her name, and again, each time louder.

"Hot." Finally, she thrashed against him. "Too hot."

Though he could barely make out her words through the shivering, he realized hypothermia had set in. Most people died of exposure like this, believing they were too warm. They shed their clothes and simply froze to death.

"No." Simon spoke firmly. "You're not hot. It's cold. Hold on to me."

"Not cold." She sounded weak, as though her body temperature had already fallen too far to bring back. "Let me up. I need to cool off. Let go."

This he ignored, clutching her even tighter. "Raven, listen to me."

At his sharp tone, her gaze focused on his face for an instant before darting away. He put his hand under her chin, forcing her to look at him. "Raven, you've got to change back."

No response. He repeated the words, louder. Finally, Raven focused on him. "Can't change back," she mumbled. "I've been having this problem lately. I've already stayed too long as wolf."

Now awake, several of her wolves had raised their heads and watched them, alert. In the small hearth, the fire embers still glowed. If he could get more wood…

At the thought, as though daring him, the wind

shook the small cabin. Going out into that storm to retrieve anything would be suicidal.

Holding her close, Simon felt when Raven's shivering all but subsided. Again, her eyes drifted closed.

"No!" He shook her urgently. "Help me here. Come on. Raven, you've got to stay awake."

"Tired," she mumbled. "Leave me alone."

Desperately, Simon tried to envelop her, to cover her smaller body with his larger one. "Change," he ordered, as by saying the word he could will her to try. The cold had gotten to him, too, and he shivered almost as violently as she had earlier.

Once she'd changed, he'd change back, too. Their heavy wolf pelts would keep them warm.

"Can't."

At least he could still hear her.

"Try again. Please." Wiggling closer, he continued to hold her close, hoping he could lend her some of his rapidly diminishing strength and warmth.

"Can't," she repeated. This time, he thought her voice sounded a little better.

Shivers racked him. Desperate to warm them both, he clutched her tightly. With a weak protest, she rubbed against him, arching her back like a cat. Despite his weakness, his body responded, his half-faded arousal roaring to life. Even so close to cold, his primal urge to mate still ran strong.

Exactly what he didn't need. Wrong, a crime, he reminded himself desperately. He had to save her life, not mate with her.

She writhed again. Against her belly, his body continued to swell and harden. He shifted his weight, trying to move that part of him away from her, but she clung to him.

Color had begun to return to her skin. Her eyes were open, her bleary gaze seemed more able to focus.

"Simon?" She breathed his name. "What's going on?"

"I'm trying to save your life," he retorted, still shivering, his arousal throbbing against her thigh. "See if you can change back to wolf now. Please."

Slowly, dazed comprehension dawned in her eyes. She attempted to push him away, a look of raw horror transforming her face as she felt his arousal. "Get away."

He continued to hold her tight, now knowing with certainty that in addition to his other crimes, the professor had raped her. "I'm holding you to give you strength and to keep you warm," he soothed. "Don't worry, I won't—"

Jaw tight, she jerked her head in a reluctant nod. Gradually calming, she focused her attention inward. "I'm ready to change."

Gradually, he loosened his grip on her, helping her get onto all fours, still cursing his unruly body.

She took a deep breath, muttered a few words under her breath and then began the process of shifting back to wolf.

Once the change had been completed, she collapsed, exhausted. Simon changed, too, then curled up by her side and slept, praying she could keep her wolf shape until dawn.

The next morning, the storm had subsided. When Raven woke, still in wolf shape, she padded over to the window and raised herself on her hind paws to peer out.

The mountain wore a heavy coating of white powder and the clear, bright blue sky promised a sunny day.

What had happened last night? Or more importantly, what hadn't happened? Simon was human, male and he'd been completely aroused. She'd been weak, helpless and completely at his mercy.

Yet he'd done nothing but try to keep her safe.

Confused, she tried to understand. He hadn't raped her, or even touched her in that way. She didn't understand.

Oblivious, Simon slept. At Raven's movement, the rest of the pack began stirring. They would all need to go outside, to roam and hunt and relieve themselves. She'd need to change back to human to open the door.

Quickly, she let the change ripple through her. Then, naked and feeling the chill, she began searching through the cabinets, hoping to find something—whether food or clothing—they could use.

All she found were some tattered old towels, a box of plastic trash bags and a dented can of beans. That would have to be enough. She wrapped one towel around her waist and tied the other over her shoulders. Then she pulled a trash bag up over each leg like a boot. A quick run outside to get enough firewood to stoke up the embers, then she'd see about finding a way to open the canned beans.

Once outside, the bitter cold hit her like a

punch to the gut. Moving as fast as she could in the powdery snow, she hurried to the woodpile and tossed aside the top snow-covered logs since they were damp. Gathering up as large of an armful as she could carry, she turned to head back to the cabin and tripped, going to her knees and sending wood everywhere.

Her limbs felt numb. Another few moments in this temperature and the frostbite that was beginning to develop would turn deadly.

Somehow, she pushed herself to her knees and raised her head. When she licked her lips, the moisture froze.

Then he was there. Simon. Human, wearing a snowsuit made entirely of trash bags.

"Come on," he urged. "Get back in there where it's warm. I'll get the wood."

Pushing her slightly, he turned and began gathering up the logs she'd lost.

For the space of a breath, she stood and watched him. Then, not about to be outdone, she went back to the woodpile and got another armful of logs. Moving carefully, she stomped back into the cabin with Simon right behind her.

They dropped their burdens on the hearth and, while Simon began trying to build up the fire,

Raven stripped off her trash bags, shivering and hugging herself. "Hurry," she told him, knowing he probably needed the warmth as badly as she.

He didn't acknowledge her words as he set up a pyramid of logs surrounded by newspaper. She noticed he took care not to use too much paper as the dwindling stack was all they had. If he was shivering from the chill, he hid it well.

Finally, a small fire crackled. Simon rose and turned to face her, stripping off his trash bags with his gaze locked on hers.

Mouth suddenly dry, Raven found herself at a loss for words. "Thank you," she said. "I owe you one."

"You're welcome." He looked away, his voice hoarse.

At his words, inexplicably her eyes filled with tears and her throat ached. She shook her head and brushed past him, crouching down by the fire and holding out her hands to warm them.

He cleared his throat. "About last night, er... this morning—"

"Don't." She cut him off, knowing she needed more time to analyze what had happened. "Can we talk about something else?"

After a moment's hesitation, he nodded. "Sure.

Let's discuss whether you're strong enough to keep your wolf shape for a few more days so we can move on."

This time, she looked away. Staring at the fire, she scratched the back of her head. "I wish I could, but I'm not like you. I can go back and forth between shapes like you do, but not if I stay wolf too long. As you know, three days is my limit. I tried, but I drained myself trying to exceed that. I need time to recover."

"How long?"

She frowned. "I don't know. A couple of days. What about the other Protector? Do you think he's close?" She hated having to ask, especially since they had no choice but to stay at least until she could change again.

"I don't know." With a wry smile, he crossed to the window and stared out at the blindingly white landscape.

"At least the storm will make it difficult for him to track us. We should be safe here for a day or two."

She swallowed, absurdly on the verge of tears. "My pack hunts without me."

His look told her he understood. "Do you want me to go with them?"

Her shrug fooled neither of them. "If you want. I think they'll accept you now."

Without another word, he went to the door and opened it. Dropping to the ground, he changed. Then, as wolf, he disappeared into the woods to find her pack.

Raven didn't know whether to laugh or cry as she watched Simon change. No exhaustion for him. When he shifted, the act seemed to be second nature. He wanted to be wolf, to hunt, so he became wolf. And left. Exactly as she longed to do and couldn't.

Chest tight, she stared after him. Then, as a blast of frigid air hit her, she moved to close the door. Human, alone, she paced the cabin, trying to understand what was happening and why.

A wave of fury swamped her. Clenching her fists, she cursed, using words she vaguely remembered from her teenage years. She was Alpha, the most powerful. She provided for her pack, for herself. She'd been content until he came along.

And now? Now she was the weakest link. Simon, a man she had to struggle to continue to dislike, had assumed the role of Alpha. Worse, she had no choice but to let him…for now. His shape-shifting skills were far superior to hers. This despite the fact that he'd been ill from blood loss. His strength irked her to no end.

She sighed. There were things he could teach her, if time permitted. Time. Since when had time become her enemy? Exhaustion rolled over her like a steamroller. Settling in front of the fire, she curled into a ball and tried to sleep.

Some time later, Simon and half of her pack returned. He pawed at the door until Raven woke and opened it, then came inside. Shaking off the snow, he lay down near the fire, letting the flames warm his fur.

Even as wolf, his masculine beauty astounded her. She studied the lean, elegant lines of him, admiring his silver-gray, glossy fur, perfect muzzle and deep-set, warm eyes.

Simon.

He cocked his head, watching her watch him. Then, rising gracefully, he padded to the door and whined, pushing at the wood with his paw.

Raven rose. When she opened the door, two more of her wild wolves padded inside. The smaller of the two, a gray-and-brown female, came to Raven and dropped a freshly killed rabbit on the floor in front of her. The other wolf did the same with another rabbit for Simon.

Stunned, Raven put her hand to her throat. By this, her pack demonstrated they accepted them both as Alpha. Only mates were usually accorded this honor. And she and Simon were definitely not mates.

Chuffing his thanks for the meat, Simon glanced away and changed. A second later, he was man again.

Startled, Raven blinked. Coherent thought vanished as he rose, naked and lithe, picked up the rabbit and began readying it to cook over the fire. All without sparing her a second glance.

"Let me do that," she told him.

"No." Still not looking at her, Simon shook his head. "You need to conserve your strength. The rabbit's for you—I've already eaten."

Though she should have been furious that he thought he could tell her what to do, she knew he was right. As much as she hated to admit it, regaining her strength so she could change and keep her wolf shape had to be top priority.

Suddenly ravenous, she didn't even let the rabbit finish cooking before plucking it from the spit and devouring it. Only when she'd picked the bones clean did she raise her head to realize he, like the rest of her wild pack, watched her.

"Thank you."

With a faint smile, he dipped his chin, acknowledging her words. "I can see you were hungry."

Though her heart had started thundering at his smile, she forced herself to keep still, to appear calm and unmoved. "Yes," she said, turning away.

"What is it you do when you change?" He asked the question in such a low voice she wasn't sure she'd heard him correctly.

"Do?" She stared at her hands, turning them over and inspecting them as though she expected to find something. Anything was better than looking at him. "What do you mean?"

"You always say something, like a prayer, right before you shape-shift. What do you say?"

"That? It's a ritual. Ever since I was small and learned I had this...talent, I asked for a blessing from the spirit of the wolves."

"Spirit of the...? What do you mean?"

She shrugged, pretending not to care. For some reason, she knew if he ridiculed her, his scorn would hurt. "Native American lore, I guess. We were studying that in elementary school and I really identified with their beliefs. They hold that everything has a spirit. I figured since I'd been allowed to become wolf, I'd better take care to appease the wolf spirit."

Simon nodded. "Okay. Makes sense now."

Now she chanced looking at him. "You believe that, too?"

"I'm not sure." A smile tugged at the corner of his mouth. "But I've heard others mention that before. Most of the U.S. pack holds to traditional Christian beliefs, but I've noticed the western half of the country tends to dabble more in other forms of spirituality. I suppose anything's possible."

Turning to fully face him, she took a deep breath. "Were you always able to stay wolf so long? Or did this ability come over time, with practice and training?"

The fire cracked, lighting the room with a flickering, amber glow. He stared at her, his eyes dark, his expression unreadable. "We learned in Protector training. This takes time and patience. Over the years, I've built up, one hour at a time."

"Great," she said glumly. "Patience has never been my strong suit."

He laughed, warming her from the inside out. "Maybe once we get past all this, I can teach you."

She couldn't help but smile back, unable to imagine even the idea that they would have any kind of a future.

Two days passed. Two long, endless days during which Simon hunted with Raven's wild pack and Raven remained in the cabin, growing increasingly sullen.

The weather continued to hold, though on the morning of the third day, the slate-gray sky and icy wind once again threatened snow.

Raven looked out the window, frowning. She'd let her wolf pack out and they'd all vanished to relieve themselves and play in the snow. Soon, they would also hunt. Without her. Simon must have known how badly this frustrated her. This time he'd stayed behind, remaining with her in the cabin.

"Simon, I think I'm all right now." She gestured at their dwindling woodpile. "We've stayed here too long. It's time to go. We need to get moving before the next snowstorm hits."

With a nod, he acknowledged the truth of her words. "The other Protector will be on the move, hunting us. You're right, it's time to move on. Do you think you can change into wolf now?"

"I'll try today. I've had plenty of time to heal."

She tried to sound confident, even though inside her stomach churned.

"Good. We'll go as far as we can, but won't stretch your endurance this time. I need you to be in good shape in case something happens."

"I want to go for three days again."

"Why? You know how badly that sapped you before."

"I'll do what I have to do," she said stiffly. "We can cover a good bit of ground in three days."

"We're stopping at two."

She gave him a sharp glance. "Fighting over who's Alpha?"

"Working as a team."

Did she have a choice? Biting her lip, finally she jerked her head in a begrudging nod. "Fine."

One brow rose. "Does that bother you?"

Shrugging, she looked away, hating how easily he read her. She'd never realized she was so transparent. "Maybe it does," she admitted. "A little."

He grinned. "Get over it."

She caught her breath, muttering half to herself. "Damn. That ought to be classified a deadly weapon."

"What?"

"Your smile." She flashed him one of her own, wishing she could knock the air from him, as well.

He gave no reaction. Instead, he started for the door. "If you don't mind, I'm going to go hunt and round up the pack. When I get back, we'll eat. Do you think you'll be ready to change by then?"

"Again you're acting like you're the leader."

He froze, his gaze sweeping over her. "We're a team, remember?"

Clenching her teeth, she stubbornly shook her head. "No, we're not a team. We're not mates. Only mates can be a team. In the wild, you have to fight me if you want to challenge me for the role of Alpha."

"Fight you?" He appeared astonished. "You really want me to fight you? Is that what you want?"

She bit her lip, staring him down, hating herself for the tight ache in the back of her throat. "I don't know," she finally said. "I'm used to being on my own."

"Then get un-used to that. It's me and you now. A team."

Unsmiling, she didn't acknowledge his words. "By the time you get back, I'll be ready to change."

With a curt nod, he dropped to the floor and became wolf. Raven let him out. She watched him as he bounded across the crusty snow, his silver coat blending with the white winter landscape.

After he'd gone, she refused to give in to the urge to cry. She had no reason to weep, no reason at all. Plus she needed to conserve her strength for the ordeal ahead.

Actually, she was glad Simon had intuitively given her time alone to attempt to change. If she failed, there wouldn't be any witnesses.

Except she wouldn't fail. She missed her pack and wanted to join them on the hunt.

Opening the door wide enough to be able to push the rest of the way with her wolf snout, she built up the fire so it would burn well in her absence.

She took a deep breath and unwrapped the tattered bedspread, her makeshift robe. Then, dropping to all fours, she closed her eyes and willed herself to change.

At first, she felt nothing. Just the beat of her heart pounding in her chest. She concentrated harder, picturing herself as wolf. A moment later, as her bones lengthened and shifted, she felt a flash of triumph. Her strength had returned, as she'd known it would.

Exhilaration roaring through her veins, Wolf-Raven padded to the door and nudged it open.

And startled the man standing on the doorstep, about to enter the cabin.

Raven didn't take the time to think—with a snarl, she launched her entire, ninety-odd pounds at the stranger's legs, knocking the man backward into the snow.

He shoved her away, pushing himself to his feet and circling the stoop, placing himself so the building was at his back.

"Feral," he snarled.

The hated word infuriated her. Baring her teeth, she bunched her hindquarters and launched herself at him again.

He kicked at her, catching her squarely in the chest, but unable to stop her momentum, which carried her past him into the side of the building.

The force of the impact dazed her. Struggling to her feet, she whimpered low in her throat, shaking her head to try and clear it. Dimly, she was conscious of the intruder, ripping off his clothes. He meant to change! This meant he wasn't merely some stranger or the cabin's rightful owner come to check on the place. He had to be the other Protector, come here to kill her.

Chapter 7

Sound traveled far in the clear, thin air. Snarls and growls, large jaws snapping the sounds of a battle. Simon froze, lifting his head. The three wolves near him did the same.

Raven! Leaving his freshly killed meal half-eaten, Simon took off for the cabin, running full-out. The other wolves did the same.

He burst from the trees, spotting the cabin. Two wolves fought in the bloody snow near the door. Raven's blood, or the other's?

Luckily, the other Protector—who else could it be?—wasn't expecting Simon. Without stopping, Simon crashed into the other wolf, sending him backward into the building. He hit with a crash and a grunt, and went down.

Simon turned to find Raven. She stood near the doorstep, sides heaving.

The other wolf struggled to his feet, leaping at Simon with a snarl.

Raven went for his hindquarters. Simon ducked low and went for the chest.

Two against one. All is fair in war, and this was definitely war.

The newcomer tumbled, rolling in the snow. In a flash, Simon was on top of him, jaw locked around his throat.

Eyes wild, the other shuddered and changed back to human.

Still, Simon did not release him.

"You won't dare kill me," the man rasped, shivering from cold or fear or both. "That would be a death sentence for you both."

Raven grinned, showing her long, sharp teeth. Simon knew what she was thinking. This man had already planned to deliver a death sentence for her.

"Let me go," their captive ordered. "Right now."

Simon didn't move. He looked from Raven to the cabin, and back, hoping she'd understand.

Dipping her muzzle, she trotted to the doorstep, then inside. Once there, she changed back to human, poking her head out the doorway.

"Let me find something to tie him with." And she disappeared inside.

Simon continued to hold on. When the man squirmed beneath him, he tightened his mouth, letting the other know if he made one wrong move, Simon would rip out his throat.

A moment later, Raven reappeared. She'd wrapped her bedspread around her and tied it, making an impromptu gown. "I found some rope in the closet. Let's see what we can do with this."

While she tied the man's hands tightly, Simon held him immobile. As she bound his feet, Simon gradually relaxed his grip.

The man began to struggle against the ties.

Quickly, Simon changed to human. "Help me get him inside."

Raven nodded and by lifting under the man's arms, together they were able to drag him inside.

"Your name?" Simon demanded.

"Heath. Heath Whearly. What's wrong with you?" The other Protector glared at Simon. "Have you gone insane?"

"Just trying to do my job."

"Do your job?" Incredulous, Heath glanced at Raven. "You've taken up with a Feral."

Raven hissed. "Seriously, I hate that word."

"A Feral." Heath ignored her. "Taboo number one in the Code of Ethics. On top of that, you've disobeyed orders. You know the law. If a Feral attacks, you must exterminate."

"She didn't attack me. One of her wild wolves did."

Heath's expression showed he didn't believe him. "Ross heard it all on your transmitter. You were taken off the case. Why are you lying for her? She's a Feral." He said the last word with a smug smile directed at Raven.

She took a step toward him. "If I ever wanted to attack someone…" She showed her teeth.

"Do it," he goaded. "Attack me. Why not? You've already earned a death sentence."

Biting back a growl, Raven shook her head and turned away.

"See?" Now Heath directed his remarks to Simon. "Ferals don't deserve our compassion. Come on, you're the Terminator, man. You're legendary. You should know that better than anyone."

"The Terminator?" Raven frowned. "What does that mean?"

Before Simon could answer, Heath did. "He's famous in the Society. We call him the Terminator because of his record number of kills." He grinned at her. "When I speak of kills, I'm talking about Ferals. In his career, Simon's killed more Ferals than any other Protector in the history of our kind."

One look at Simon's face, and Raven knew Heath was telling the truth.

"Were you really sent just to kill me?" she asked.

"I was sent to evaluate you." His expression gave nothing away.

"And then kill you," Heath put in.

"Not necessarily," Simon shot back. "I really think she can be rehabilitated."

With a snort, Heath shook his head. Despite the situation in which he now found himself, he didn't seem too worried. His arrogance made Raven dislike him even more.

"Have you ever rehabilitated a Feral?"

"Of course I have." From Simon's thunderous expression, he'd like to throttle the other man.

"How many?" Raven asked, keeping her gaze on Simon, amazed that she managed to sound so calm. "How many have you saved and how many have you killed?"

Heath snickered.

"I don't want to talk about that."

Odd how she felt so betrayed, by a man she barely knew.

She opened her mouth. "But—"

"Not now."

As she prepared to argue, Heath pushed-jumped, propelling his body up. Though his hands and feet were still bound, he launched himself at Raven.

Startled, Raven tried to spin out of the way, but she was too slow.

Heath hit her hard. They fell, she scrambled to get out from under him. With a snarl of triumph, Heath changed.

Simon slammed him over the head with a log. Instantly limp, Heath's body reverted back to completely human.

Shuddering, Raven pushed the other man's inert body away, managing to get out from under him.

"Is he…?"

For both their sakes, she hoped not.

Carefully, Simon approached, his adrenaline still pumping. "He's not moving. I don't think I hit him hard enough to kill him."

Kneeling, he felt for a pulse. When he located

one, he flashed Raven a relieved grin. "Not dead, thank the hounds. Killing another Protector is not only an automatic death sentence for me—"

"Like mine, you mean?"

"I'm trying to rectify that." He continued with his previous sentence, as though she hadn't spoken. "And worse, once I'm branded an outcast, no one will listen to anything I have to say about you."

She crossed her arms, looking mad enough to spit glass. "Aren't you already an outcast?"

Staring at her, he was appalled that she would even think such a thing. "Of course not. This is all just one big miscommunication. I can fix everything, once I get them to listen to reason."

"Assuming they'll listen to you."

"They will." He made his voice confident. Fumbling in the other man's backpack, he located the transmitter, noting that Heath had snagged one of the newer digital models.

Taking a moment to study the black plastic box, he sighed. Then, using the same log he'd wielded to take Heath down, he smashed it to pieces. "That felt good."

Raven nodded, apparently unappeased.

He kept digging through the full backpack.

Finally, he found one of the Society's special cell phones. "Exactly what I wanted. Perfect," he said, holding it up so she could see.

"What are you doing?" Raven crossed her arms. "Those things won't work up here."

"This one will. I'm calling in." Punching in the numbers from memory, he listened as the phone at the other end rang.

A moment later, Ross answered. "Did you find them yet, Whearly?"

"This isn't Whearly." Simon grinned, imagining his boss's reaction. "Though he was kind enough to loan me his phone."

"Caldwell. That explains why the signal went dead. You disabled the transmitter." Ross sounded furious and tired. "The screen just came up with an untraceable signal."

"I had to." Simon took a deep breath. "I want you to reconsider. Let me finish this assignment."

"Finish?" Ross made a strangled sound. Simon could picture the veins bulging in his forehead. "You've been taken off this case, Caldwell. The Society is calling a meeting later this week to decide whether you should be permanently removed from our roster."

Simon couldn't conceal his shock. "Removed

from the roster? I haven't killed anyone. Isn't that a little extreme?"

"You've disobeyed a direct order. On top of that, you've been placed on involuntary leave." His boss took a deep breath. "What have you done to Whearly?"

Simon glanced at the other man. "He's unconscious. He came up on the losing end of our fight."

"Adding assault to your other charges?"

"Other charges? What the hell is wrong with you? I've done nothing wrong. Come on, Ross. Call him off. I'm fine. I'm a damn good Protector and you know it." Simon gripped the phone so hard his knuckles showed white.

Ross changed his tone from furious to concerned. The switch was so contrived and obvious, Simon nearly laughed. "If you're fine," Ross pleaded, "then come in. Let the Society be the judge of your mental state. You're our star Protector. We don't want to lose you. We're all worried about you, Caldwell."

The words were calculated as a balm to his wounded ego. Simon set his jaw. "I can't come in. You know that. I have a job to finish."

"No. You. Don't," Ross enunciated slowly. "Come in now."

"Absolutely not."

"See? You've now received another direct order, which you chose to disobey. You're off the case. End of subject."

Glancing at the still-unconscious Whearly, Simon took a deep breath. His boss was usually much more reasonable, which meant someone else, someone higher up, was putting pressure on him. But why? "Come on, man. You have the power to reinstate me. Put me back on the case. Let me finish what I started."

"Are you going to exterminate the Feral?"

"Hell, no." Simon answered without hesitation, watching Raven nibble on one fingernail. Every time he looked at her, her fresh-faced beauty and athletic grace continued to amaze him. "If you met her, you'd understand."

"Hellhounds," Ross swore. "So that's the reason you're doing this. I never pegged you for someone who'd violate the Code of Ethics."

"I haven't." Simon knew he sounded defensive. "And I won't. That has nothing to do with it. You know me, Ross. Cut me a break here."

"Fine. But Caldwell, I don't care if she looks like a *Sports Illustrated* model. She's Feral. She attacked you. She's got to go."

"No."

"Then tell me why." The frustration in Ross's voice wasn't fake. Since the transmitter had already given their location, he didn't have to bother tracing the phone call, so there was no reason for him to keep Simon on the line.

"She's done nothing wrong. I swear. I wouldn't lie about something like this. I believe in our organization. What we do is necessary and right. But I also thought we were fair and just. Every damn thing that's occurred since I phoned in to make my first report has been contrary to that."

He took a deep breath. "Ross, I'm good at what I do. You know that. In my years as a Protector, I've never asked for anything. Not once. I'm asking now. Let me finish this case. I honestly believe Raven can be rehabilitated."

Raven's head snapped up at the mention of her name. Scowling at him, she shook her head.

"Raven?" Ross asked. "Is that what the Feral calls herself?"

For the first time in his life, Simon, too, was beginning to hate the word *Feral*. He was sure as hell tired of hearing it applied to Raven.

"Yes," Simon answered, keeping his voice

even and professional. "She's sane. And smart, too. She's suffered some abuse at the hands of that professor in Boulder."

"The one who was just murdered?"

"Yes." Briefly, Simon filled his boss in on Raven's story. When he finished, he reiterated his plea. "You've got to let me finish this case."

"No. I don't have to do anything, other than make sure you're rounded up. We're very worried about you."

"You're being completely unreasonable."

"We are not unreasonable." Ross sounded highly offended and exasperated. "You have always been one of our most highly regarded Protectors."

"Then give me another chance. Give *her* another chance."

Ross chuckled. "I think I now understand why you're defending this Feral. That's another crime against you, you know. One more and we can order *your* extermination."

Simon's mouth dropped. He was glad Ross couldn't see him. "I've never heard of such a thing." His voice was icy calm. Deadly. "Are you making your own rules now, Ross?"

"We know where you are," Ross warned.

"Traveling with that pack of wild wolves makes you easy to track. Plus, we have the transmitter's last recorded location. We'll send reinforcements. More than one, this time."

"More than one." Simon gave a bitter laugh. "I suppose I should be honored."

While Ross was still sputtering, Simon disconnected the call. What Ross had threatened went beyond his realm of experience. In all his time with the Society, he'd never heard of a Protector being exterminated. That couldn't be legal. Not to mention moral or ethical, or any of the high standards the Society espoused.

He had no choice but to suspect corruption. Starting with Ross.

Heart heavy, he dropped the cell phone in his pocket. One more check on Whearly revealed the other Protector was still out.

"We need to get out of here before he wakes up," Raven said, her voice flat.

"I agree." He gave a quick nod, glancing at the window. "How soon can you be ready?"

"My wolves are still hunting. You'll need to give me time to gather my pack. Is that okay, *Terminator?*"

Hellhounds. "Raven, wait." He touched her

arm, knowing they didn't have a lot of time, but wanting to explain anyway. "The ones I killed, I only did what was necessary."

"Sure you did." Giving him a look of pure disgust, she brushed off his hand. "Keep telling yourself that, why don't you? I'm sure Whearly here would do the same, once he succeeded exterminating me."

"We don't have time for this. Call your wolves in and get ready to go."

Jerking her head in an angry nod, she turned to do just that.

"Raven, you need to think about letting them go."

"Who?" From the doorway, she looked back at him blankly, not comprehending.

"Your pack. They'll be safer away from us. We'll be safer, too. Traveling with so many wolves makes it more difficult to find places to hide. Not to mention making us more visible. Ross even mentioned it."

She stiffened. "No. Absolutely not."

"Think about it for a minute. Too much depends on us staying ahead of the Society. Ross said he's sending a team. Keeping away from one determined Protector is difficult enough," he said, indicating Whearly. "But since Ross is sending more, with your pack in tow it'll be damn near impossible to evade an entire search team."

She gave him one final mutinous glare and opened the door. Lifting her human face up, she howled, sounding eerily like a wild wolf. "That should bring them back. And no, I'm not getting rid of them."

"We don't have a choice, Raven. Not if we want to live through this. We've got to get rid of your pack. Temporarily," he added for good measure. "You can always collect them later, once this is over." *If* they survived, that is. He kept that to himself.

Blinking, she shook her head. This was an instinctive reaction, done without thinking. He gave her an additional minute to process his words, knowing he was right.

"I'm their Alpha." Her protest was weak, and he suspected she knew it. "They won't be able to function without me."

"Designate a new Alpha. You know how it goes. The one that attacked me would be a good choice. Chase him or her off, then the others. They'll follow the other one then."

"But they won't understand."

"You're humanizing them. They're wild animals. They won't understand anyway."

Seconds passed while she stared at him. Finally, she dipped her chin. "You're right. I've got to let them go. But it doesn't mean I have to like this."

"We'll do it on the run." He indicated Whearly. "I don't know how long he'll be out."

When he saw her beautiful eyes fill with tears, he had to clench his fists to keep from going to her.

"We have no time," he urged, to make her turn away.

Predictably, she did. "We can't just abandon them. They'll try to find us."

"And you'll chase them away."

"What if they come to the cabin? What about him?" She pointed at the other man. "What if he hurts them?"

"He'll have no reason to, unless they threaten him."

Back stiff, she shook her head. "I can't take the chance. Look what happened with you. I won't endanger my pack."

"Then gather them up. We've got to get moving. We've got to put as much distance between this place and us as possible. But your wolves are going to have to go if you want to have a decent chance of surviving this. You can chase them away on the run."

"You made things worse. Get rid of the cell phone. Don't call those people again."

He hid a smile at the way she still tried to give him orders. "I'm going to hang on to it. You never know when we'll need it. There are a few other people I want to call. For now, we've got to put as much distance as we can between this place and us."

Finally, she nodded. "Change, then." Her voice was harsh. Dropping to the ground, she shape-shifted back to wolf. Panting, her glossy black sides heaving, she crossed to the door, waiting for him to pull it open.

"Just a minute," he said. "I want to rig a way to carry this phone with me when I'm wolf." Grabbing one of the trash bags, he placed the phone inside, then tied a knot. With a few twists and another knot, he made a sort of trash-bag collar, placing it on the ground in front of him.

She watched silently, no doubt thinking him a fool.

"When I'm wolf, I should be able to slip my snout through this and wear it."

With a shake of her furry head, Raven trotted over to the plastic bag ring. She nudged it once, then made a low, chuffing sound. Extending her head, she pawed at the bag.

"You want me to put it on you?" Simon couldn't keep the shock from his voice.

She woofed again, indicating agreement. Simon picked up the collar and slipped it over her head. It fit loosely enough that she should be able to slip her head out of it before she changed to human next time, but well enough that it wouldn't fall.

Again, Raven padded to the door, waiting for him to open it. He did, and then, not wanting to leave Whearly tied, he went to the still unconscious man and loosened the bonds. Once he'd finished, he dropped to the ground and changed to wolf, too.

Though her howl had summoned two or three wolves, most of her pack was still out hunting. Padding away from the cabin, Raven let out a long howl, then another. The sound was totally different from that she'd made while human.

Even as wolf, especially as wolf, listening, he felt a chill go through him.

She howled a third time and they began to appear. First one, then another, traveling in small groups, rarely alone, her wild pack assembled.

He didn't know how Raven knew when they were all there, but when she turned to him, apparently satisfied, and gave a quiet woof, he realized she was ready to move on. He let her lead the way, following close on her heels.

The rest of the pack fell in behind them, content to follow.

Chapter 8

Slogging through so much snow wasn't easy, even as wolf. At least the slow pace gave Raven time to think. The plastic, trash-bag collar felt unfamiliar and slightly uncomfortable, but carrying the cell phone made her feel as though she was doing her part, at least.

Too bad about Simon. Until now, she'd thought him honest, intelligent and kind. She'd believed his good looks weren't all he had going for him.

She'd actually begun to like the man until she'd learned of his horrible nickname. The Terminator. On top of that, he then informed her she needed to get rid of her pack.

Simon had no idea what he asked of her. Her wild wolf pack had become her family and she loved them, each and every one.

Part of her understood his logic. A large group was always more difficult to hide than a small one.

But her wolves—oh, her wolves.

The first snowflakes began to fall when they'd been traveling a couple of hours. Beside her, Simon touched his snout to hers. She knew what he wanted. She just didn't know if she could.

Gradually, the snowfall increased, approaching near-whiteout conditions. They were lucky there was no wind. If this much snow had been blowing, they would have been completely unable to see. As it was, the snow fell heavy and silently, decreasing visibility to a few feet.

The temperature began dropping, as well. Though she had no way of gauging it, Raven guessed they were in the lower teens, inching backward toward zero.

This time, Simon bumped her with his shoulder, hard. Baring her teeth, she told him to back off even though she knew he was right.

They needed to find shelter soon.

The wolves sensed this, as well. Instead of ranging out from Raven and Simon as they normally did, they drew together, in herdlike formation. One, a young male she'd called Theo, crowded her too close and nearly knocked her down.

She would begin with him. Heart heavy, she turned and bared her teeth at him, snarling and snapping, chasing him from the pack.

Bewildered, uncertain, he ran to the edge of a nearby group of trees, clearly intending to shadow them while remaining on the pack's fringes.

The snow kept falling, a curtain of white ice.

Without warning, Raven spun in the snow and attacked another. Teeth bared, she chased three, then four, of her wolves away, watching as they ran toward Theo, where they formed their own small pack.

Without her.

Not allowing herself to think, she went after the others. None of them fought back. She'd so sturdily established herself as Alpha, they were used to doing as she dictated.

Soon, all the wolves save she and Simon waited with Theo at the edge of the trees.

Giving them one final look, Raven leaped

forward, attempting to bound across the snow. Simon kept pace with her, though she suspected he found movement more difficult due to his weight. He sank much deeper into the crusted powder than she did.

Of course, her pack attempted to follow, though they kept distance between them.

Raven ran back, struggling in the snow, and chased them off. She did this three more times before they stopped following.

Night had begun to fall when she saw the last of her wild wolves, watching from a distance. As she and Simon made it up another hill, they began to howl, saying goodbye and mourning their loss.

The wretched sound pierced Raven's heart. If wolves could have cried tears, she would have wept. All she could do was continue on, with only Simon at her side until they could find someplace to take shelter. She knew her former pack would do the same.

Abruptly, Simon changed direction. Instead of heading up the mountain, he began traveling downward, keeping close to a half-frozen stream. Raven had no choice but to follow, though she wasn't sure she agreed with his choice. She wasn't familiar with this area and had no idea

where they were going. As darkness fell and the
snow continued falling, she could only hope they
found shelter soon. Otherwise, she'd find a big
tree and dig her own shelter through the snow, in
the ground until she'd made a den. She'd done
this before and made it work, so she had no doubt
she could do it again.

Simon stopped, causing her to nearly collide
with him. He nudged her, using his snout to
indicate below. She looked, trying to see through
the snow, and once she saw the twinkling of ar-
tificial lights she realized he'd led them toward a
human town.

Why? Did he honestly think they could take
shelter there? She looked at him, considering.

After another nudge, this time with his
shoulder, Simon began moving forward, down,
closer to town.

Thoroughly chilled, Raven finally followed.

Halfway up the mountain, they came to a ski
lift. Near the lift were several buildings—one
marked Equipment Rental, a restaurant/bar, a
small storage facility and a ski shop. All were
closed for the night. With this kind of powder,
they'd all open at first light, ready to accommodate the hoards of skiers.

Like two wolves coming this close to civilization wouldn't be noticed. Or, if they changed, two naked humans freezing in the snow.

Still, trusting Simon's instincts, she followed.

At the ski shop, Simon paused. Then, shaking the snow off his fur, he rose on his two hind paws and peered in the window.

Though the swirling snow made seeing difficult, below them the lights winked out. The entire town lay dark, without power. The storm must have knocked it out. If the ski shop was alarmed, the alarm wouldn't work now.

Simon trotted away from the ski shop. Then, running, he hurled himself at the wooden door. The door shuddered, but the frame still held.

He went back for a second attempt. Raven joined him. Together, both wolves rammed the door. With a crash, the wood splintered, creating an opening wide enough for them to get in.

Getting up, Simon shook himself, then nudged Raven to precede him. She did, moving gingerly. When she'd slammed into the door, she had felt like she'd bruised her shoulder.

Once inside, where the solid wood walls kept out the frigid wind and snow, Raven realized they'd entered a treasure trove. There were ski parkas and ski pants, insulated shirts and slacks, boots and socks and shoes. In short, everything a human would need to keep warm in the snow. Dressing in these clothes would be as warm or warmer than her wolf fur. Plus, changing to human would give her a respite from being wolf.

Slipping her head from the trash-bag collar, she worked it with her paws until she was free. Then, she changed. A moment later, Simon did the same.

Human again, naked and cold, she couldn't stop shivering. Her teeth chattering, she looked around, trying to decide which clothing to take.

As she grabbed a soft, turtleneck shirt, Simon came to her. Pulling her into his arms, he gathered her close.

At first, his cold, clammy skin did nothing to warm hers. They shivered together. And she found herself gripping him as hard as he gripped her, holding the forgotten shirt loosely in her hand.

Finally, finally, she began to feel heat as the blood flow returned to her limbs. Teeth still chattering, she attempted to speak. "Why here, in town, I mean? Why human?"

"The other guy will be looking for us up there." He jerked his head toward the mountain.

"They're also sending reinforcements, a search party. I don't know how many more will come. The last place they'll look for us will be here in town."

She could feel his heartbeat, steady and strong, against her chest. Her nipples, already hard from the cold, burned and she had to suppress the urge to rub her breasts against his chest.

Warmth spread to other parts of her body, as well. She felt her lower body grow heavy and wet. Her breath caught, her heartbeat accelerated. To distract herself, she swallowed and asked the first question that came to mind.

"Where are we?"

From the slight hitch in his breathing, she knew he'd noticed her arousal. "I'm not sure."

"Grab some clothes and get dressed. If we're going to stay human a while, we've got to get out of here before the resort opens in the morning."

They dressed hurriedly, choosing clothing for warmth. Both selected light-colored parkas, knowing that for now, they didn't want to stand out in the snow.

"I've never stolen anything like this," Raven said, feeling absurdly guilty as she zipped up her jacket and placed a pale blue ski cap on her head.

"What about all those campers?" he reminded her. "You stole from them."

"Used stuff." To her, there was a big difference. "From clotheslines and trash bins and garage sales. I never broke into a store and took new clothes."

"Me, either. But it's a matter of survival right now. Later, when I'm able, I'll come back up here and leave them money for all this."

"You know the police will be looking for us now, too."

"I know." He sounded grim. "And we'd better hope the power doesn't come back on while we're in here. I'm not sure what kind of alarm this place has, but I think it will notify them. That's why we'd better get moving."

"Where are we going to go?"

He laughed, the short bark of sound almost as chilling as the snow. "I don't know. There are lots of vacation homes in the foothills before town. I'm guessing we should be able to find at least one empty. We'll stay there for now."

"Breaking and entering again?"

His hard stare softened as he looked at her. "I don't see that we have a choice. Unless you have an alternative plan?"

She shook her head. "No." She sighed. "I don't." Bracing herself to go back out into the storm, this time as human, she zipped up her jacket, adjusted her cap and pulled on a set of ski gloves. She thought about asking him about his plans after—did he plan to continue living day-to-day, always on the run—but decided not to Part of her thought she really didn't want to know.

"Are you ready?" he asked. She saw he, too, had closed his coat and pulled on his gloves.

"I guess." Starting toward the hole in the door, she turned to face him. "You know what? I just want my life to return to normal. Is that too much to ask?"

He shook his head, his eyes dark and completely unreadable. Moving jerkily, as though against his will, he reached for her, placing a single, firm kiss on her lips before letting her go. "I'm sorry, Raven. But you may as well resign yourself. I don't think your life will ever be normal again."

He left her staring after him as he went out the door.

Trudging through the snow as human was ten times more difficult than as wolf. Weighed down with all the subzero clothing, as she slogged

through the snow behind Simon, Raven had
ample time to think. And worry.

Once again, Simon had shaken her to the very
core. She worried about the way he was able to
do that to her with merely a touch, whether of his
hand or his lips, or even a look out of those dev-
astating dark eyes. She feared letting him, letting
anyone, have that much power over her. Her life
had been just fine until he came along.

Then why couldn't she shake the sense that she
was lying to herself?

Simon. Always back to Simon. She found him
far too beautiful. Even as wolf his form was
welcome to her lupine eyes. She dreamt of him,
obsessed about him, and in general felt like a
young girl with her very first crush, which in a
way, she was.

Everything she wanted now revolved around
him.

Adjusting her woolen ski mask over her face,
she sighed. She felt a great fear that she had become
too accustomed to having Simon around. Part of
her wanted to test that theory, to order him away,
while the other part, the aching, forlorn, lonely part
that she so despised for its weakness, wanted to
clutch at his arm and beg him never to leave.

This she would never ever do. She hoped. She didn't know if she worried more than she should have, or if she didn't worry enough.

Simon stopped and she ran into him, making him stumble a step forward. He didn't comment, no doubt aware she wouldn't hear him over the ferocity of the storm.

Instead he pointed.

Squinting, she looked in the direction he indicated, seeing nothing but snow. Finally, she saw the barely discernable outline of a house.

At her nod, Simon moved forward again, bent into the wind. Putting her head down, Raven followed.

Though the storm was fierce, Simon felt as though the fates had smiled on him yet again. They were safe for now. No one could travel in the mountains in such a blizzard, and the snow would hide his and Raven's tracks.

Though Raven appeared unconcerned, she really didn't understand how the Protectors were. Ross's threat really worried him. Alone, Protectors were excellent trackers. When they worked together in a group, nothing and no one could hide from them. It was only a matter of time before they were found.

The sole advantage he and Raven had right now was the weather. That, and the fact that he was banking on their searchers assuming their prey would remain in the mountains. Their descent into town should buy them a bit more time.

He turned, checking as he did every few minutes to make sure Raven was still right behind him. If he'd thought of it earlier, he would have roped them together. If she were to wander out his sight, it would be hell finding her with the visibility near zero.

But she kept pace with him, though her shorter stride made trudging through the deep snow more difficult.

The day wore on and the icy wind continued to gust, sending swirls of white to blind them, and the temperature continued to plunge. When darkness fell, anyone foolish enough to be caught outdoors would risk their lives. The sooner he found shelter, the better.

The first house they found was occupied. They gave it a wide berth, continuing down the road. They bypassed several other houses, even though they were empty. He wanted something not too accessible, yet with a view, enabling them to see anyone approaching, yet hidden enough that it would be easily overlooked by searches.

Finally, tucked around a curve, down a long driveway and perched on the edge of a cliff, they located a small, A-frame cabin that appeared to be deserted.

This time, he didn't have to break down the door. The homeowner had left it unlocked. As the door swung open he and Raven exchanged a glance. He wondered if she'd had the same fleeting thought he'd had, worried this might be some sort of a trap.

But how could it be? Their pursuers had no idea where they'd gone.

Stepping inside, Simon flicked on a switch.

"No wonder the door was unlocked," Raven said dryly. From the looks of things, the A-frame hadn't been occupied in quite some time. A film of dust lay over everything, from the chipped and discolored kitchen counters to the torn and dingy furniture. There were two plastic lawn chairs in the living room, along with a torn and faded sofa that sagged in the middle. The place smelled musty and dirty.

"Yeah. There's nothing in here to steal." Simon couldn't keep his gaze from returning to Raven.

Her nose twitched adorably while her expression mirrored her disgust.

"I'd rather live in my cave than a place like this."

She made him chuckle. "Chin up. At least it's shelter from the storm. We won't have to stay long."

Making a quick tour around the room, she shook her head. "What kind of person would live here?"

Watching her, he marveled at her graceful walk. Even half-frozen, the woman still embodied femininity. To his disbelief, his still-chilled body stirred.

Ruthlessly, he tamped his desire down. This had been happening way too often lately. It had to stop. Despite what Ross might think, Simon would never ever break the Code of Ethics. Not even for a Feral as beautiful as Raven.

If only he wasn't having so much trouble thinking of her as Feral.

"What a dump," Raven said again.

Glad of the distraction, he agreed. "Must be a guy's place."

"I pity his wife, though looking at this place, I doubt he has one. Or if he does, I don't think she's ever been here."

Tending to agree with her, he grinned. "Yeah. Lucky for us, the owner doesn't appear to live here."

"I should hope not." She sounded horrified. "This has got to be a vacation house, though he must not use it for skiing."

"Maybe he stays here in the summer or fall. It has the look of a hunting cabin."

"It has the look of a pigsty."

"At least we don't have to worry about anyone walking in on us." Laughing, he felt obliged to point out the positive. He liked the way Raven could make him smile, even in a situation like this.

She didn't appear to know what to make of his amusement. "Walking in on us? Like anyone could travel in this storm."

Smile fading, he took a deep breath. "Protectors can."

She gave him a hard look, opening her mouth as if she meant to say something scathing. Instead, abruptly, she closed it and nodded. "Then we'd better keep moving. Once the storm passes, I mean."

"Yeah. Though the snow is to our benefit."

"Whatever. I'm sick and tired of winter," she said.

"Me, too. Next time they send me on assignment, I'm going to make sure they send me some place tropical."

"*If* they send you on assignment." She shook her head. "After all that with your boss, I'm thinking you've got to start trying to decide on another career."

He didn't comment. They were both cold and exhausted.

Instead, he watched while Raven prowled around the kitchen, still battling his inexplicable arousal. Amazing that he could be this cold, this exhausted and starving, and still want her.

Opening one kitchen cabinet after another, finally she shook her head. "All empty. I think you might be right about the time of year they use it."

"I'm right?" he teased, unable to resist. "Must be a red-letter day."

The joke earned him a quick smile.

"Do you need to eat? If we need to, we can always change and go hunting." Though he really didn't want to go back into the cold, changing might actually help dispel his growing arousal. At least until he changed back.

Still unaware of his discomfort, she glanced at the window, dark save for the white of the storm swirling outside. "I'd rather go hungry than go back out into that."

He nodded in agreement.

A set of stairs led to a loft, no doubt where they'd find the bed. Assuming there was a bed. He could only imagine what kind of mattress would be in a place like this. Absurdly, even thinking the word *bed* made him harder.

Raven returned from making another circle of the room, hugging herself. "I don't see a thermostat, so I'm guessing there's no heat."

Glad of the distraction, he walked the perimeter of the room. "You're right. I'm thinking we'll have to use that woodstove to heat the place."

"At least he has a pile of wood stacked under that tarp." She pointed.

He got busy collecting wood. The physical activity helped him get his mind, and body, from the gutter. Still oblivious, she puttered around the place, searching out cupboards and closets.

Once he had a nice fire going, which was enough to make a dent in the cold, they unzipped their coats and pulled off their hats and gloves. He tried not to look at her, uncomfortably aware of their solitude.

With a sigh of pleasure, she went and sat cross-legged in front of the fire. He joined her, careful not to sit too close.

"What now?" she asked. "I did what you

wanted and got rid of my pack. So what are your plans? Where do we go from here?"

He pulled Whearly's cell phone from his pocket. "First, I want to call someone else, a friend of mine. He's another Protector, though he's on vacation right now. I'm trying to remember his number." He thought he had most of it, except for the last couple of numbers. In that case, he'd try different combinations until he hit the right one.

With a shrug, she returned her attention to the fire.

The phone screen was blank. Frowning, he held it up. "No signal. Maybe it's the storm."

"Or the battery is dead."

Surprised, he checked the screen. "No, right now it's got plenty of charge. Though I'd better conserve it." He touched the power button and the phone went off. "I didn't take the phone's charger. I wish I'd thought of it, but I considered myself lucky to even get the phone." Snapping the cell closed, he stuffed it back into his pocket.

"Yeah." Unsmiling, she watched him. "So, what now?"

What now? For the first time in his life, he'd acted impulsively. He hadn't thought far enough ahead. Normally, he planned everything. Now, because they were on the run, living day-to-day, he could plan nothing.

Raven shifted her weight restlessly, startling him out of his thoughts.

"What's it like, being able to stay wolf for so long?" She didn't bother to try and keep the envy from her voice.

He glanced at her sideways, then shrugged. "Normal. Second nature."

"Better than being human."

Silently, he digested that. Her last statement was at the core of what made her Feral.

Evidently his silence prompted her to ask another question. "You really like living among humans?"

He raised his head. Now this comment was classic textbook in the Society. His training held that if a Feral ever made a remark showing interest in an assimilated life, they were definitely able to be rehabilitated.

Never before had he met a Feral so contradictory.

"Yeah. At least, better than this." He glanced around the tiny cabin. "I have a soft bed, hot showers, all the food I want." He shook his head. "But you know this. You said you occasionally stay in Boulder."

Her gaze skittered away. "I spent all my time frightened."

Now she'd startled him. "I don't understand."

When she swallowed, he saw the movement in her slender throat. "People have hurt me in the past."

In that simple statement, she gave yet another hint to her past. Yet it was something, better than nothing, and he made sure to be careful to ask his question in a soft voice.

"The professor?"

She nodded. "Mostly. But there have been others. Boulder's a dog-friendly town. How do you deal with the domestic animals' reactions?"

For a moment he wasn't sure he understood. "You mean they—"

"Sense what I am. Most of them don't like it. Their eyes see human, but their noses tell them I'm wolf. I've been attacked at least six times."

Now he understood. "That's easy to correct. It's all in the way you walk, the way you present yourself to them. I forget sometimes you weren't raised among shifters. We're taught at an early age how to blend in."

She made a sound, part grunt, part sigh. "You

can't tell me that every single shifter, and I believe you said there were thousands worldwide, receives training."

"The one raised in a pack environment do. Of course, not everyone is brought up in our lifestyle."

"Exactly. What about those? How do they cope?"

He had no idea. "Maybe they know instinctually how to deal with pets. I do know that this particular issue is rarely a problem."

"It is with me." She gave him a sad smile. "That's why I find life easier living away from society. Even as a child, I never fit in."

"You didn't know there were others like you."

"No. But I still wonder how like me they really are."

"Any difficulties can be overcome with training." He winced, aware he sounded like he was reading directly from an advertising brochure. Once, he'd believed everything he'd been taught wholeheartedly, without reservations. Now, looking at Raven's haunted, beautiful face, he wondered how much he really knew.

He really needed to talk to Beck. He said so out loud.

She sighed. "Why are you so obsessed with these people?"

He gave her a sharp glance, but saw only curiosity in her face. "These people, meaning my job?"

She nodded.

"My job has always been my life. The Society is very select when they choose Protector candidates. I left my family when I was four and went to live in a dorm. From that point on, everything I thought, said or did was directly related to being a Protector. Without that…"

"You think you are nothing." Her soft comment made him wince.

Finally, he nodded.

"Have you ever known anyone who's done what you did?"

"Disobeyed an order?" He thought for a moment. "Actually, no."

"And you claim I live a sheltered existence. Just because you've never heard of it, doesn't mean it never happens."

"True," he admitted, though he found the idea unpalatable. "But if that's the case, then the fact that no one ever speaks of it isn't good."

She frowned. "What do you think happens?"

Saying the words out loud felt like blasphemy,

but he said them anyway. "I'm beginning to think they're exterminated, just like a Feral who can't be rehabilitated."

"That would make you, all Protectors, nothing more than—"

"Murderers."

Chapter 9

The blizzard continued on until late the next afternoon, depositing more than a foot of heavy powder. Forced to wear her human form so long, Raven felt antsy. Part of the reason was the close proximity to Simon and the unsettling effect he had on her.

For so long, living as close to a wild animal as she could manage, her desires had been simple. Food, shelter, the companionship of her pack and sleep. Anything she wanted, she took.

But she'd never craved anything the way she had begun to want Simon. Fighting this constant desire made her snappish, with a bad case of cabin fever.

After her comment about Protectors being murderers, Simon withdrew even further from her, brooding and pacing and muttering under his breath. She left him alone until she could stand the silence no longer, then made a small comment or two, hoping to start an argument.

Nothing worked. He ignored her, not seeming to even notice the confinement, not appearing to mind being trapped in the tiny chalet with her. When she spoke, he grunted an answer. He treated her, she thought with disgruntlement, like an annoying younger sister. Perversely, this only made her want him more. She'd never been one to pass up a challenge.

In fact, while the blizzard raged outside, she felt more and more trapped, contemplating changing and heading outside. Only the intensity of the storm stopped her, because even wild things had to hunker down when the weather got this bad.

Her furious restlessness finally got Simon's attention.

"What is wrong with you?" he asked, watching her wear circles in the worn and faded rug.

"I don't like this." She delivered her answer, the understatement of the century, in a surly tone. "I'd rather keep moving."

"Me, too, but not in that." Gesturing at the window, he smiled, causing her stomach to do flip-flops. "We have no choice but to wait this out."

The first night, Simon let her have the bed and tried to sleep on the sagging couch. The second, he told her they should switch, but he couldn't do that to her. No one could sleep on that couch, he'd said.

"I hope you don't mind if I share the bed with you?" The last he delivered with a rakish grin.

All she could do was stare. Her throat had gone dry, and she knew if she tried to speak, her voice would come out in a croak. She licked her lips, wishing for lip balm.

"I—" she finally managed.

His grin faded. "I didn't mean like that," he said quietly. "Just for sleep. I won't touch you, I promise."

"I'll take the couch." She turned away so he wouldn't see her conflicted emotions in her face.

"No. Listen, I'm sorry." He reached for her, touching her shoulder.

In the interest of self-preservation, she flinched away. "Don't touch me."

Narrow-eyed, he watched her, lowering his hand. "What's wrong with you?"

"I was raped." The words felt as if they were torn from her.

"Yes, I know. By the professor."

"Over and over and over." Closing her eyes, she tried to blot out the images, but she couldn't. She wouldn't cry, couldn't cry, she'd wept over all that too many times in the past, and she was done crying for something she couldn't change.

But now Simon reached for her, and heaven help her, she couldn't move. At first. Then, she found herself struggling, blindly striking out, terror and rage filling her as she tried to get free.

He wouldn't let her go.

"Shh," He held her, murmuring soothing sounds, over and over until she ceased struggling and stood frozen, feeling like a captive rabbit, trembling in his arms.

"I won't ever hurt you," he whispered, smoothing her hair, his touch gentle, his voice soft. And suddenly she wanted more. More. Damn it. Much more. She wanted things she had no right to want. Things she had every right to want. His touch, washing away the stain of the past, cleansing her body, fulfilling her...

With a soft cry, she pushed him away. This time, he let her go.

"You take the bed," he said quietly from behind her. "I'll sleep on the couch."

Ashamed, aroused and feeling more than a little sorry for herself, Raven turned without a word and climbed the stairs.

The next morning they danced around each other, skittish as strangers. When the snow finally stopped falling, Simon opened the door to two feet of fresh powder.

"We should have taken skis."

As an attempt at a truce it was pitiful, but Raven was so tired of the silence, she said the first thing that came to mind. "Can you ski?"

He glanced at her. "You never learned?"

"No." She sighed. "Maybe if we had snow-shoes…"

"We've got to get going. The Protectors won't let a little thing like this deter them. We've got to go."

"As wolves or humans?" she asked.

"I think we'd better stay human." When she frowned, he held up his hand. "We're going farther down, maybe even as far as Boulder Canyon. They won't think to look for us if we travel closer to civilization."

Despite her reluctance, his logic made sense.

"Can we change before we leave and go for a hunt? My wolf," she touched her chest, "is restless."

This brought another of his achingly beautiful smiles. "Mine, too. Sure, let's change. It'll be good to let our wolves out."

Raven didn't wait to hear anything else. Stripping off the hated, yet warm clothing, she cracked the front door open, dropped to the floor and changed. She ran out the door in a flash of black fur, leaving Simon behind.

Simon supposed he should be glad Raven was so skittish. He didn't know why he'd proposed they share the bed, which would certainly have been a test of his self-control. Trapped in such close proximity to Raven, he'd found the temptation overwhelming. He'd had to mutter the Code of Ethics to himself several times, each time he looked at her and his body stirred.

The instant the words left his mouth, he regretted them; even more so when Raven had begun freaking out.

Changing to wolf would be a huge relief.

Shedding his clothes, he dropped to the floor to begin his own change.

She waited for him by a grove of trees, her compact body coiled as she prepared to spring into a run. As he neared her, she took off. Grinning, he gave chase.

As he plowed through the snow, Raven's black wolf-self barely ahead of him, Simon felt all his worries melt away. Sensation flooded him—the cold, powdery snow under his paws, the sun warm on his fur, the icy breeze promising plentiful game and a fair winter day.

His muscles flexed, powerful, working in unison in a way his human body never would. He leaped, simply for the pure joy of the movement, and when he landed he sent up a powdery plume of snow.

A second later, Raven did the same, though she jumped at him. Hitting him hard, she rolled him in the snow, playfully snapping.

Much larger than she, he pushed back, rolling her not once, but twice, then standing over her with his tongue lolling. His stance dared her to try to move him and being Raven, of course she did.

Scooting out from under him, she tucked her hindquarters and ran, skimming the snow. Four wolf lengths away, he caught her and sent them both tumbling down a hill.

While running with his own pack, Simon had seen other wolves play in a similar manner, though in small groups rather than one-on-one. Such play between two wolves was reserved for mates. Though Simon knew this (and suspected Raven did, as well), his wolf took too much pleasure in the lupine play to care.

As he and Raven circled each other in preparation for another tumbling match, somewhere to their left a wolf screamed.

Instantly, both he and Raven froze.

The sound came again, piercing. Simon had only heard such a scream once before, when a wolf had gotten gored by an angry elk.

The cry had come from a small grove of trees to their left. Glancing once at Raven, Simon immediately took off in that direction, running at a full gallop.

Raven followed, gaining ground rapidly until she was close on his heels.

Together, they burst into a small clearing. There, the snow was red with blood. One of her wolves, Theo, the young male who'd refused to leave her, shrieked again. He must have followed them. A black metal bear trap had closed around his back leg.

In the space of a heartbeat, Simon changed back into human. Barefoot and naked, he hurried to within a few feet of the trapped wolf. Raven, knowing the quick shifts back and forth would cost her, also became human and grabbed his arm.

"That's Theo. One of mine. He's in pain and he doesn't know you. Let me."

He gave a curt nod. "You'll have to hold him without getting bit. It's gonna hurt like hell when I go to pry the trap apart."

"I know." Murmuring low in her throat, she approached the injured wolf. Out of his mind with pain, the young male snarled and snapped, narrowly missing Raven's arm.

Naked in the snow, they both shivered. "We need something to wrap his leg. We've got to stop the bleeding."

Nodding, she changed back to wolf and took off for the cabin. Since they'd left the front door open, entering shouldn't be a problem.

Waiting, Simon changed to wolf himself since he'd be warmer. He kept a safe distance between him and Theo. The young male was in excruciating pain, snapping, moaning and grunting. Every now and then he let out an agonized cry, which pierced Simon's heart.

After what seemed an eternity, Raven returned. Still wolf, she carried what looked like a pillowcase in her mouth.

When she reached him, she changed to her human form, immediately shivering. She held out the pillowcase. "This should be enough to use for a tourniquet."

Simon changed back, too, dreading the instant slap of cold, especially on the bottom of his still-numb feet.

"Are you ready?"

At her nod, Simon eyed the whimpering wolf. "You've got to hold him still while I get the trap off." Simon knew he sounded grim. "Maybe you should try to subdue him as a wolf rather than human."

"It'd sure be warmer."

"Yes." He glanced at the ever-widening blood staining the snow. "We've got to hurry before he goes into shock and I freeze. I've got to get that thing off and the wound wrapped before he loses too much blood."

He didn't tell Raven that the wolf would most likely lose his leg. He could only hope the trap wasn't rusty. Without a way to sterilize the wound, the risk of infection ran high and the young animal would be lucky not to lose his life.

"Good idea." Again, Raven instantly shifted into her wolf shape. Simon turned his attention to the young wolf. Weakening from the blood loss, the gray-coated wolf shuddered, struggling to keep his head up, snapping and snarling at nothing in particular.

Issuing a low growl of warning, Wolf-Raven crossed to Theo's side. She lowered herself slowly until the bulk of her lupine body sprawled across the injured wolf's torso, pinning him down. Each time Theo raised his head, she bared her teeth. Because she was his Alpha, he finally gave up.

Now. Simon went to the trap. Made for bear, the heavy iron trap appeared to have been set and forgotten. It looked old and rusty. His heart sank.

He glanced once more at Raven. Then, satisfied she'd be able to keep the young wolf from lashing out at him in pain, Simon began prying apart the rusted metal, his blood-covered fingers freezing.

The instant he got the trap open, the nearly severed leg began spurting blood. He packed the wound with snow and ice and wrapped the tourniquet tightly on the upper leg.

"I wish we had some pain meds and antibiotics." He swore fiercely. "This is worse than I thought. Raven, if you want this wolf to live, we're going to have to go into Boulder. I grew up there and one of my best friends is a vet. He'll help us."

She stared at him, her wolf eyes unblinking.

"Help me get Theo into the cabin."

Watching the tenderness with which he tended the young wolf, Raven knew a moment of doubt. Though she kept trying to force herself to see Simon as the evil Terminator, his actions constantly surprised her.

Though she hadn't asked, she didn't understand why he'd bothered to help the wild wolf. Taking care of the injured animal would slow their progress by days, maybe even weeks. From the way he'd talked about Ferals, wild wolves should mean nothing to him, but he never once considered abandoning the wounded animal.

She could almost *like* the man for that.

Especially since she would have refused to leave Theo. For him, she would venture into town.

A few hours later, Simon had rigged a sled using plywood, some old two-by-fours and rope.

"We'll take him down the mountain on this," Simon told her.

They dressed silently, each eying the wounded

wolf. Theo had lapsed into a fevered unconsciousness, but their attempt to lift him had him
snapping. Finally, Simon had to place a makeshift
muzzle over his snout.

Together they lifted the injured animal onto the
sled. Theo let out a moan, then a grunt, before
lapsing back into unconsciousness.

Simon took the left rope, Raven took the other.
Pulling the sled together, they headed down
toward Boulder.

Daylight had begun to wane by the time they
finally rounded a turn and saw Boulder stretched
out below them.

The injured wolf still lay unconscious on the
rough sled they'd made, his shallow breathing
and weak heartbeat testifying to the urgency of
the situation.

"Where's your vet friend located?" Raven asked.

He withdrew the cell. Now he had plenty of
signal. "Let me call him."

"Wait." She touched his arm. "Is he in your
Society?"

"The Protectors? No. He's a friend, just a guy
I went to college with up in Fort Collins. He's
not pack."

Glancing at him, she raised a brow. "I

thought you said the Protectors took you when you were four."

"They did. But we weren't kept in a compound or a monastery. We were sent to foster homes, in a community where other Protectors lived. It wasn't until I was put on active duty that I had to go live in headquarters. It's kind of like the human military, I guess."

She nodded. "Are you from here, then?"

"Born and raised. I grew up in Longmont."

She hadn't known he was a Colorado native. Nor that the Protectors had apparently allowed him to have some semblance of a normal life. But then, why should she?

Simon made the call, talking in a low voice. When he finally closed the phone, he gave her a thumbs-up. "I filled him in on what's been happening. We can bring Theo to his clinic. He'll meet us there."

"Great." But she couldn't make her feet move.

"Are you ready?" He seemed to understand her fear.

"I grew up in Boulder," she told him, careful to keep her voice neutral.

"Yeah, you told me. You went into town to steal food and supplies."

"Not that town." The words came out in a rush. "Nederland, maybe even as close as Golden, but not Boulder. Never Boulder. Too many bad memories there." Though she'd mentioned her fear before, she thought she might have understated how she really felt. Terror might be a better description, if her pounding heart, tight chest and trembling were any indication.

She wanted to change back to wolf and run, far away, back to her pack, away from him and the city stretched below them, lights twinkling like stars. Boulder. The place where her torture had begun.

Only the knowledge that Theo needed help kept her from doing so. Theo was part of her pack. As Alpha, she had to make sure he was taken care of.

"Are you all right?" he asked.

"Hmm." She made a noncommittal sound, then stood frozen in place when he started moving forward, letting the sled rope slip through her gloves.

He got about forty yards away before realizing. Turning, he cocked his head. "Aren't you coming?"

For the life of her, she didn't know what to say. She'd given her word that she'd try, but that had been when everything was an abstract, a remote and distant concept rather than actuality. Going into town to steal and run was one thing. Staying there was another. Now, faced head-on with her worst fear, she didn't know if she was strong enough to overcome it, even for Theo.

"I…"

Leaving the sled, he came back to her side. "Don't be afraid." Slipping his arm around her shoulders, he pulled her close in a quick hug. "I'll be with you."

Just like that, her fear vanished. Odd, that he had this effect on her. She wasn't sure if she liked it. Matter of fact, she knew she didn't.

Chin held high, she stepped forward, grasped the sled's rope and headed forward, side by side with Simon.

He glanced at her as they walked. "The professor's dead, so there's no reason to be afraid."

"I know." Struggling to find the right words, she gave up and shrugged instead. "I can't explain how I feel, or why. Boulder doesn't hold good memories for me."

"It can't all have been bad. What about your life before the professor? What was that like?"

"My childhood?" Considering, she chewed her bottom lip between her teeth and trudged along beside him.

"What about your parents?"

"I only have vague memories of them. They were killed in a car crash when I was five." She shot him a glance, her throat unaccountably tight. "I have flashes of memory. Sometimes I still remember my mother singing to me, rocking me in a giant white chair."

"That's good that you remember her. I was taken from my mother when I was four. I never saw her again."

"Taken? By the Protectors?"

"Yes. Over the years, I've tried to locate her, but either they paid her well to stay hidden, or something happened to her. I've never found her. And unlike you, I don't remember her at all."

She winced. "I'm sorry. When I think of my mother, I feel love. Unconditional, deep love."

"What about your father?"

"My father I remember more as a voice— deep—and big hands."

"But they both were shifters?"

"I don't know. I didn't even know there was such a thing until I saw you." Her dry tone was self-deprecating. "So no, I have no idea."

"At least one of them was. Do you heal quickly when you're hurt?"

She nodded. "Why?"

"Full-bloods do. Tell me more about what you remember from your past."

The cold, thin air made it difficult to walk and talk. That, and as usual she felt the impact of his grin. She paused to get her breath.

After a moment, she continued. "Like I told you before, after my parents died, Child Protective Services took me in. I was placed in foster care. Maybe that's why the professor knew no one would be looking for me."

They'd come full circle. Back to the professor. She hated that everything in her life always did.

She sighed. "Anyway, I was adopted by one of my foster families when I was seven. Life was good for a while. We lived in the foothills near Thompson Canyon, in a small log cabin. They were kind of hippies."

Again that flash of a grin. She shook her head, as if she could shake off his effect on her. "You're a good listener."

"Thanks."

"You're a captive listener, too." She managed to smile at him, wishing her smile would knock him to his knees the way his did her.

Of course he just kept on walking, pulling the sled behind him.

After a moment, she continued. "I kept my changing secret. I'd wait until everyone was sleeping and sneak out, becoming a wolf and roaming the mountains. Those were happy times. One day, I returned home to find my new mom waiting for me. She'd discovered my empty bed when she'd heard a noise and come to check on me."

He glanced at her, but said nothing. She guessed he was letting her tell the story at her own pace.

"I thought I might have to explain, make up some story about meeting friends to drink in a meadow or something like that, knowing she'd understand. But instead, she told me she'd followed me. She'd actually *seen* me change."

"Hellhounds." Glancing at her, he grimaced. "How did she react?"

"Actually, quite well. She was fascinated. She went to the Boulder library and checked out a bunch of books on lycanthropy and werewolves. She gave them to me to read."

He growled low in his throat. "Most of those books are all wrong."

"It didn't matter." She lifted one shoulder in a

shrug, changing the sled rope from her left hand to her right. "Since werewolves weren't real, none of what these books had to say mattered. I thought I was the only one, a freak of nature. But my adoptive mother accepted me. Loved me." Even to this day, the knowledge awed her.

"So life was good?"

"Yep. I was happy. But then my mother, Flo, got sick," she continued, her expression carefully blank. Coming to this part of her story, her nerves resurfaced. Suddenly, she didn't want to look at him, so she stared at the road ahead. "Traffic's light this time of year, isn't it?"

Simon refused to take the bait and change the subject.

"Things got bad for you after that?"

"Mike, my adoptive dad, had always used recreational drugs. His usage escalated when his wife got sick. After Flo died, he decided I could become…" She took a deep breath. "Her substitute."

"How old were you?" Simon sounded hoarse, as though appalled.

"Fourteen. I ran away the first time a few months later, when I turned fifteen. The police brought me back after two days."

"You know, you make me want to try to find

Wild Wolf

this Mike and rip out his throat. Why didn't you tell the police or someone? Surely they would have helped you."

She lifted her chin, aware her expression was a study in blankness. She'd perfected that look at a teenager. "Why? So Child Protective Services could come and get me? I didn't want to go back into foster care. The stuff that goes on there is just as bad, sometimes worse. No, thank you."

"So you stayed and put up with his—" Simon swallowed.

"I stayed. But I made sure Mike never touched me again."

"How?"

Her slow smile contained no trace of humor. "I changed. I let him see my wolf, and made it quite clear if he touched me again, he'd die."

"If I could let go of this sled, I'd applaud," Simon said. The steepness of the incline would have made letting go of the rope dangerous. "I'd have done the same thing if it'd been me."

"Yeah." She didn't know what else to say.

"So he left you alone and let you continue to live with him. Then what did you do?"

"I endured as long as I could. Planning to escape, to go live on my own as soon as possible.

But what I didn't know was that good old Mike had begun scheming of a way to use my special abilities to get money." She couldn't keep the bitterness from her voice.

"Get money?" He squinted at her, frowning. "You mean like a carnival show?"

"Worse." She took a deep breath. Though she faced him, her gaze was very far away, in the past. "That's how I came to be with the professor."

"What?" Simon sounded shocked. She supposed she couldn't blame him. "He—"

"He sold me to the professor. And, as you know, I was kept in one of those cages in the back of the lab."

A muscle worked in his jaw and then he looked away. Raven wondered what he was thinking, if he somehow blamed her for what had happened the way she sometimes blamed herself.

The silence was broken only by the sound of their footsteps, the sled scraping the snowy pavement and the harsh sound of their labored breathing.

Finally, she could stand it no longer. "Simon?"

When he turned to look at her, she saw the fury burning in his eyes. "If you were to tell me now that you killed that man, I honestly wouldn't blame you."

She took a deep breath, the ice cold that had been spreading to her heart abating. "I didn't, but I would have liked to."

"Me, too," he said. "Me, too."

More and more houses began to appear. Finally, they reached the extreme western edge of Boulder. Traffic grew heavier and when they saw an RTD bus, Raven knew they were in town.

"We've got to head north." Simon pointed the way.

If anyone found two people towing an unconscious wolf on a makeshift sled strange, they didn't stop to comment.

The vet clinic, in an unassuming cinder block building, sat in an out-of-the-way cul-de-sac off Thirtieth Street. Like so many of the buildings in this area, it had been built in the fifties and touched up with beige paint to try and make it look modern. A small sign proclaimed Dr. Zachary Archer, DVM. Since the clinic had already closed for the day, the parking lot was deserted except for a battered, dark blue Tahoe. Since the parking lot had been plowed, they kept to the still-snowy grass and headed around to the back.

As Simon lifted his hand to knock on the door, two men with black ski masks rushed around the building, rifles drawn and aimed at both Simon and Raven.

Chapter 10

Simon didn't think. He dove at the closest man, knocking him down before he could fully bring his weapon to bear on Raven.

As the second man spun to bring his gun to bear on her, the back door of the vet's office opened, yellow light spilling out into the rapidly darkening night.

Raven yanked off her coat and dropped to the ground. Her clothes tore, splitting along the side seams.

Wolf again, she snatched up her parka with

her teeth and took off running, low to the ground and zigzagging, trying to avoid the spray of shots.

"What the…?" Then, without hesitation, Zach Archer, DVM, jumped the second man, knocking the rifle from his grip. Head-butting the guy, Zach knocked his opponent's head into the concrete step, knocking him unconscious.

Zach then grabbed the rifle. "How come every time I run into you, Simon, there's trouble?"

Still wrestling with the first man, Simon grinned. He got in a lucky punch just under the guy's chin. While the man reeled from that, Zach brought the rifle down on the back of his head.

"Thanks. Nice to see you, too." Climbing to his feet, Simon grabbed the other gun. "How the hell did they know to find us here?"

Zach shrugged. "How do they know anything? Besides, don't you guys wear transmitters or something?"

"No. Not now. All I've got now is a cell phone."

"There you go. Satellite maybe?"

Simon sure as hell hoped not. If the Society could keep that close a tab on him, he was doomed. "Where's Raven?"

"The woman that shape-shifted in front of

these goons?" Zach's brows rose. "She took off that way."

Since what Raven had done was technically against pack law, Simon knew he should tell his friend that Raven was Feral. But eyeing the other man, Simon honestly didn't want her classified that way. So he said nothing, instead directing his friend's attention to Theo.

Instantly, Zach dropped to his knees beside the wounded animal. "Christ." He whistled. "The leg's going to have to go."

Rising, he dusted off his pants. "We need to get him inside. But first, what do you want to do with these two guys?"

"I don't know. Normally, I'd call pack police. But since I'm not sure what's going on with the Society right now, we'd better tie them up and bring them inside, too."

"What about the woman?"

Simon had been eyeing the direction in which Raven had vanished. "I'm hoping she'll come back as soon as she realizes it's safe. Otherwise, I'll go look for her."

Zach laughed. "Now there's a story I'm dying to hear. After we get this mess cleaned up and I get the wolf stabilized, you can start talking."

Once the men were securely tied up, they deposited them in an old storage building in the back of the property. While they were finishing this up, Raven returned, still in her wolf shape, skulking around the snow-covered bushes until they closed the shed door.

Simon hid his relief. Until that very moment, he hadn't known if Raven would use that opportunity to disappear into the foothills. The fact that she hadn't made him want to hug her.

Oblivious to his inner turmoil, Raven paced the perimeter of the yard. Then, she crossed to Theo, who'd begun thrashing about. Zach ran inside and returned with a syringe. "This will knock him out for now. We need to move him into the surgery and get an IV into him."

"We'll have to carry him." Worried, Simon eyed Theo's leg. Blood had soaked the makeshift tourniquet.

"I've got something we can slide under him. It's like a triage stretcher." Zach broke off talking and whistled. "Your lady friend just changed back to human. That's one good-looking woman."

Before he thought better, Simon bared his teeth at his friend. He bit back a single word— *Mine*.

Still gazing at Raven, Zach didn't notice.

Simon turned, too, watching as she gathered up her torn clothing and tried to dress herself.

He itched to assist her, but knew she wouldn't welcome his help. Once she'd finished dressing, she walked over to where the two men stood.

Eyeing Zach, she indicated Theo. "Will you be able to help him?"

Unaccountably flustered, Zach nodded. "Let me go get that stretcher," he said, and disappeared inside.

"Thanks for coming back." Simon touched her arm.

Her bright blue gaze met his. "You thought I wouldn't?"

Staring down at her, all he could think about was how badly he wanted to kiss her. "I wasn't sure," he said, his voice sounding like gravel.

Zach returned before Simon could say anything else. Or, he admitted to himself, do anything utterly, completely foolish.

Once Theo had been moved inside, Zach chased them out of the operating room and closed the door.

"What now?" Raven whispered, exhaustion raw in her face.

He wished he knew. "We take things one day

at a time, Raven. One day at a time." Starting with what to do about the Society's goons. If those two had been able to find them, that meant true Protectors weren't far behind.

An hour later, Zach emerged from the room, wiping sweat from his forehead. "It's gonna be touch and go," he warned them. "I've pumped him full of pain meds and antibiotics. All we can do now is monitor him and wait and see."

Raven slumped against Simon. Putting his arm around her slender shoulders, he helped her stand.

"You two look worn-out." Zach smiled. "I'm guessing you need a place to stay?"

Simon nodded. "Just for tonight, okay?"

Glancing at his watch, Zach pulled out his cell phone. "Let me call one of my vet techs to come up here and keep an eye on the wolf. Then we'll head out to my place. I live over by the hospital, so it's not far."

He made the call, talking in a low voice. Simon held on to Raven, feeling like a drowning man, but unable to keep from enjoying how good having her lean on him felt.

Closing the phone, Zach eyed the two of them and smiled again. "Are you ready? By the way,

another friend of yours came by the other day."
He sounded casual, too casual.

Simon could tell from his expression that his
friend was worried. "Who?"

"Anton Beckham."

"Beck?" Shocked, Simon dragged his hand
across his jaw. "I was just telling Raven I
needed to talk to him. He's supposed to be on
vacation. I figured he would be in Mexico or the
Caribbean."

"Well, he's not. And he looks like hell, almost
as bad as you two do."

"Why? What's happened?"

"All I know is, first him, now you. Something's
seriously messed up in the Society. But I'll let
Beck tell you himself. He gave me his cell phone
number. We'll give him a call later."

The vet tech, a sleepy-eyed college student who,
with his hair standing up in tufts all over his head,
appeared to have been roused from a deep sleep,
showed up a few minutes later. After Zach gave
him instructions, they all headed for the Tahoe.

Once outside, Zach stopped. "What do you
want to do about the two goons?" he asked, indicating the storage shed. "We can't leave them
there overnight."

"Why not?" Raven sounded savage. "They attacked us."

"Maybe you should call the police." Simon slipped his arm around Raven's shoulders, pulling her close. "File a report, press charges, all that. Tell them these guys were breaking and entering, etc. Let the Boulder Police Department deal with them."

"Boulder PD? Not pack?"

"Not pack. We can't take a chance until we know what's going on with the Society."

Zach nodded. "We'd better go back inside. It's warmer there."

They waited in the clinic waiting area while Zach made the call. "They said they'd be here in a few minutes." He sounded cheerful and full of energy, something. Simon could only hope for. Maybe after a few hours of sleep he'd feel that way, too.

When a police car pulled up in front of the clinic a few minutes later, Simon cautioned Raven to stay inside. He and Zach went out to meet the officers.

Twenty minutes passed while the officers took their report. Zach led them to the storage building and opened the door. Still trussed like turkeys, the two men glared at them. With their black ski masks and clothing, they looked like criminals, and the policemen had no reason to doubt Zach's story.

One officer began reading the two their rights. The other slapped handcuffs on them. Once they were cuffed and their rights read, the officers bundled them into the squad car and they sped away.

Tired and cold, Simon went inside to get Raven. "They're gone. Let's go."

"Aren't you worried about what they'll say?" Raven asked, walking with him back outside. Zach waited by the Tahoe, keys in hand.

"No. They're shifters and they won't break pack law. They won't tell the humans anything."

"How do you know that? They're bad guys. What do they care about the law?"

Simon shook his head. "Pack penalties are much more harsh than human. Remember, we're half wild animals." He hoped she wouldn't ask for more specifics.

Raven narrowed her eyes. She opened her mouth and Zach interrupted.

"Even if they did tell their story," Zach put in, "who's going to believe them? Werewolves? Protectors? Ferals? People would think they were crazy."

After a moment, Raven nodded. She rubbed

her hands together to warm them. "So we don't need to worry about them anymore, right?"

Zach unlocked his vehicle and they all piled inside. Once Raven had buckled in, Simon did the same. He'd like to have kept his arm around her, but there was no reason to inside the SUV.

Zach started the engine. "Let's give it a moment to warm up, then I'll turn on the heater." He glanced at his vet clinic, frowning.

"You still look worried," Raven pointed out. "Why?"

Zach sighed. "I'm concerned. Somehow they knew you'd come to my clinic."

"True," Simon said. "Good point. I hadn't thought of that."

"I wonder how they knew." Raven rubbed her temples. "The wolf…"

"The wolf," Zach echoed. "What do you think is the chance they set the trap that injured your wolf?"

Simon exchanged a glance with Raven. "I hadn't thought of that. Maybe they were trying to catch one of us."

"And caught Theo instead."

"Theo?" Zach put the vehicle in Drive and they moved forward. "You named a wild animal Theo?"

Simon couldn't help laughing. "What do you expect from a Feral?" he said, laughing even harder when Raven punched his arm.

Zach lived in a modest, raised ranch, perched on a small rise at the end of a dead-end street. "Here we are," he said cheerfully. "Don't mind my dogs."

About to get out of the vehicle, Raven froze. "Dogs? What kind?"

"Boxers." Zach caught the look on her face. "Why? What's wrong? My boxers are a hundred times more friendly than wild wolves."

"Raven doesn't like dogs," Simon said.

Thinking he was joking, Zach laughed. "A shifter who doesn't like dogs? Right."

Face devoid of expression, Raven hung back.

"You're serious?" Zach asked, glancing from Simon to Raven and back.

"Afraid so." Simon crossed to her side of the vehicle and slipped his arm around her shoulders, unaccountably warmed when she sighed with relief and slumped into his embrace.

"Let me put them out back." Still shaking his head, Zach unlocked his front door and went inside. Standing on the sidewalk, they could hear the boxers' enthusiastic greetings.

Raven shivered. "I don't know why I'm so afraid."

"I don't, either," he teased, squeezing her shoulder. "You've lived with a pack of wild wolves for a few years. What's a couple of seventy-pound boxers to that?"

For that remark, he earned a smile. Tentative, to be sure, but her smile made him feel like the sun had just broken through a slate-gray, stormy sky.

From the doorway, Zach laughed again. "Come on, you two. I've put the dogs out back for now, though you'll have to get used to them sooner or later. I only have one guest bedroom. I'm guessing that won't be a problem?"

"I can take the couch," Simon said without thinking.

"No." Raven's fingers dug into his arm. "Don't leave me tonight. Not here, not like this."

Swallowing, Simon nodded. Maybe she didn't understand that they'd have to share a bed. Perhaps once she saw the room, she'd understand why he'd offered to spend the night somewhere else. Anywhere, besides lying next to her. He didn't know how much temptation he could take.

Maybe she didn't realize how badly he wanted her. The time they'd spent together, both as wolf and as human, hadn't lessened his desire. If anything, his craving for her had increased. He now spent almost every waking hour aroused.

As they crossed the threshold into Zach's bachelor-decorated house, he hoped she'd fall asleep before he did. Then he would sneak off to find his rest elsewhere. That would be his only chance of getting some sleep that night.

Outside, darkness fell swiftly. Zach showed them their room, and then led them to the kitchen where he pointed at his glass-topped, round kitchen table. "Sit. I'll make something to eat. But first," he glanced at Raven, "the temperature's falling and my boxers have thin coats. They aren't used to the cold. Are you ready for me to let them in?"

Though she stiffened, she nodded, trying unsuccessfully to hide her unhappiness at the idea.

"Remember, just act normally," Simon told her in a low voice. He reached for her hand across the table and squeezed.

She squeezed back, then pulled away. "I'm not sure I know how."

Shaking his head, Zach went to the back door

and pulled it open. Two stout boxer dogs bounded inside, jumping up and down, stubby tails waving furiously. One was a reddish-gold color and the other was a mahogany brown, so dark he almost looked black.

After leaping into the air and joyfully greeting Zach, they rushed over to inspect the newcomers. Since Simon sat closer to the door, they sniffed him out first. He held perfectly still, holding out one hand.

"Just like with wolves, don't look them in the eye," he cautioned Raven.

"And loosen up," Zach chimed in, eyeing the way Raven sat stiff, like a statue. "They won't hurt you."

True to his word, the largest of the two animals sniffed Raven, then licked her hand. The other followed suit. Then, apparently satisfied, they retreated to huge, pillowed dog beds on the other side of the kitchen.

Raven let her breath out in a loud sigh.

"See?" Zach beamed. "I told you they were harmless." Then, winking at Simon, he went to the fridge and began assembling ingredients on the counter.

"Are you guys hungry? I make a mean stir-fry."

As if on cue, Simon's stomach growled. Even Raven laughed.

"I'll take that for a yes," Zach said, still grinning.

They sat at Zach's glass-top kitchen table and watched while he made pork stir-fry in his wok.

"That smells amazing." Raven lifted her chin, sniffing the air. From the beds on the other side of the room, the boxers did the same.

When Zach finally set two heaping plates in front of them, Raven and Simon exchanged a glance. Then they both dove in, devouring all their food before Zach had even halfway finished his.

"There's more," Zach pointed. "Finish it off."

So they did. After, while Zach stacked the dishes in his spotless, stainless steel dishwasher, Raven nodded off.

Watching her, Simon couldn't help but smile indulgently.

"You've got it bad, old pal," Zach commented. "I've never seen you like this."

Simon frowned. "Don't be ridiculous." The sharp glare he sent his old friend worked to discourage him from saying anything else. He didn't know why, but talking about his feelings, whether real or imagined, for Raven would be dangerous.

Asleep, Raven slumped down in her chair, head

on the table. One of the boxers, ever curious, crept closer, finally jumping up and licking her cheek.

"Ahh!" Jumping, she woke. Glancing blearily around her, she gave the dog a faint smile. "I think that's my signal. Do you mind if I use your shower?"

"Not at all." Zach smiled. "There are plenty of towels inside the cupboard."

"Thanks." With a slight wobble, she walked back to the guest bathroom, closing the door behind her with a quiet thump.

"If she wasn't yours, I'd try for her." Zach's tongue-in-cheek comment made Simon take a deep breath. He hadn't even realized he'd been holding it.

"She's not mine," he replied automatically. Then, rubbing the back of his neck, he gave his friend a sheepish smile. "There are rules about Protectors and Ferals. No way I'd break one of those."

"But then, you're not actually a Protector anymore, are you? At least, it doesn't seem so after what you've told me."

"Once a Protector, always a Protector." Again, his answer came without thinking.

"Dude, they're trying to *kill* you. You saw those guys. I bet they had silver bullets in those guns."

Simon cursed. He hadn't thought to check for that. "We should have looked before we let the police take them."

"Maybe. But what are you going to do?"

"Raven's been asking that question, too. You know, I really don't know. Until those two guys attacked us, I thought I could convince my boss to let me finish my assignment."

"Beck said this was supposed to be his assignment. That you had him taken off so you could have it instead."

Simon grimaced. "I had him taken off because I thought he was talking crazy. Now, I'm beginning to think he wasn't."

He glanced at the clock on the microwave. "You said you have his number. Would you mind giving him a call? I'd like to talk to him."

Without another word, Zach flipped open his cell and scrolled through his address book. He punched Send and then tossed the phone to Simon. "Here you go."

Beck answered on the third ring. Instead of answering with his last name as he usually did, he simply said hello.

"Beck. It's Caldwell. Where are you, man?"

"Why?" Hostility. Simon should have expected that.

"Look, I'm sorry. I had no idea. I thought I was doing you a favor by having you sent on vacation."

"Vacation?" Beck snorted. "I'm not on vacation, that's for sure. More like on the run for my life."

"What? Why?"

"I bucked the system. Normally, no big deal, right? But Ross has turned the Society into the Gestapo. He's gunning for anyone who doesn't behave like a robot."

"Which explains why he's gunning for me," Simon said.

Silence while Beck digested this. Then, "You? What the hell have you done? You've always been their shining example, the model Protector. The Terminator." This last was said with so much bitterness, Simon winced.

"Can you help me? I'd like to figure out what's going on."

"I want to ask you a question." Beck's voice cracked as static came over the line, then the static faded. "You've been there longer than me. How connected in the Society is Ross?"

"Ross? I don't know. He's been there a long time."

Beck coughed. "Look, talking like this on the cell isn't safe. You don't know who might be listening. I know where you are. I'll be over there in half an hour."

Before Simon could respond, Beck hung up.

Shaking his head, Simon handed Zach the phone.

"Well?" Zach dropped his cell into his pocket. "What's up?"

"He's on his way here." Simon tried to rub the grit out of his eyes. "I sure wish I knew what the hell is going on."

Zach chuckled. "Maybe you're about to find out."

When the knock came at the back door a few minutes later, to their credit the boxers didn't bark. They harrumphed twice, watching Zach. Satisfied that they'd done their canine duty, they settled back in their beds when he crossed to the door to open it.

The tall, angular man who entered bore little resemblance to the man Simon had sent on vacation just a few weeks ago. The man looked ten times worse than he had the last time Simon had seen him and recommended him for a mandatory vacation. With the dark circles under his eyes, hollow cheeks and close-cropped hair, he looked like a walking cadaver.

"Beck." Simon stared in shock at his friend and former coworker. "What the hell happened to you?"

"Sit down before you fall," Zach advised, pointing at the chair across the table from Simon. He went to the fridge and got them each a beer.

"I can't stay long," Beck protested. "They're after me. If I stay too long in one spot, they'll find me."

Simon popped the top off his beer and took a long swallow. "Sit your ass down. What the hell are you talking about? Who's after you? I think you'd better explain."

Hesitantly, Beck sat. Simon slid a beer across the table to him. With a sigh, Beck opened it and took a sip.

"The people after me are the same people that are after you."

"Protectors? Why? Did you defy a direct order?"

"Is that what you did?" Beck leaned forward. "Because when I told them I sure as hell didn't need a vacation, Ross sent goons after me. He wants blind obedience. I think he's trying to form his own army."

Frowning, Simon took another drink. "That doesn't make sense."

"I don't know," Pulling out the third chair, Zach sat. "There've been rumblings for a while now about a big shake-up in the World Pack Council. Maybe your Ross is going for that."

"World Pack? I thought we were just talking about the Society. The World Council is several notches up from that."

Unblinking, Zach watched him. "Lesser men sometimes have lofty political expectations."

"Oh, it's worse than that." Beck slugged back a third of his beer, wiping his mouth with the back of his hand. "He's eliminating anyone who questions his orders. He's gone from eliminating dangerous Ferals to eliminating dissenters."

"I still don't understand." Simon's head had begun to ache. "The Society is well respected in the pack. Even if Ross succeeds in assembling his own bunch of brain-dead Protectors, what does he plan to do with them?"

"This is what I've been trying to find out. I'm not sure how high up this conspiracy, for lack of a better word, goes. I've attempted a bunch of times to contact someone higher up in the Society. I've been blocked at every turn."

"Who? Who have you tried to call?"

Simon and Zach watched as Beck ticked off the names on his fingers.

"So now I'm calling Turley."

"Turley?" Simon whistled. "Hellhounds."

Zach looked from one to the other. "Clue me in, guys. Who's Turley?"

"Turley is on the Supreme Council of the Society. That's our governing body. He's in charge of the entire organization and of all the Protectors. Ross is peanuts compared to him."

"Kind of like comparing a senator to the president?"

"Exactly." Both Simon and Beck nodded.

"In the meantime, Ross has a crew after me," Beck said.

"Yeah, me, too. You know the Feral you were assigned before you got sent on mandatory vacation?"

"Yeah, the job you worked?"

"Ross wanted me to exterminate her before I even filed my report. I refused, so he sent a replacement. Raven and I—Raven's the Feral—went on the run. It's all gone downhill from there."

One of the dogs raised his head and woofed. The other got up, padding toward the hallway that led to the guest bedroom.

"I thought I heard another voice." Barefoot, hair disheveled, Raven wandered into the kitchen, her long hair wet. Though she wore clean clothes Zach or someone had placed on the bed, no doubt leftover from a girlfriend, they were too big and she'd wrapped a blanket around her like a serape.

"That felt wonderful." Though she smiled, her blue eyes were slightly unfocused, and she covered her mouth gracefully with her hand as she yawned.

Simon thought she looked unbelievably gorgeous.

"Beck, meet Raven. Raven, this is Beck, a friend of mine."

Beck stared, openmouthed, as Raven tilted her head to look at him. "*This* is your Feral?"

"I hate that word," Raven scowled. "Please don't use it again around me."

"Uh…okay." Beck rubbed his eyes, continuing to stare. "You look… Were you a captive of a professor a few years ago, here at CU?"

Crossing her arms, Raven slowly nodded. "How did you know that?"

"Because there was another one, another girl who looks just like you. Ross has pulled out all the stops trying to find her. The last sighting of her was a video taken by the professor a couple of months ago. Ross wants her, dead or alive. There are standing orders that she's to be captured or exterminated on sight."

Chapter 11

"Exterminated?" Raven wrapped her arms around her middle. "You people never cease to amaze me. Why do you want to kill her? Because she refuses to live by your rules?"

Beck set his jaw as a flash of anger lit his gray eyes. "First off, I'm not *you people*. Second, they're not *my rules*. Not any longer. I'll offer you a truce, Raven. I won't call you *Feral,* if you don't lump me in with the ones who want to kill me. Fair?"

Slowly, Raven nodded. "You're right. I'm sorry."

He accepted her apology with a nod. "Did you know about the professor's other captive?"

"Simon told me there was another girl." Raven watched as Beck took a long drink of his beer, finishing it. He placed the empty bottle in front of him and leaned back in his chair, crossing his arms. Like Simon, he radiated masculinity. Unlike Simon, he looked rough, as though he perpetually strolled on the edge of a crumbling cliff.

"Information on her was in my report, but I didn't know she looked like Raven," Simon said. "Nor was I privy to the bring-in-or-kill order. That must have gone out after I left for my assignment."

"You mean *my* assignment," Beck grumbled, one corner of his mouth twisting up in a semi-smile. "You grabbed it."

"You said you were burned out." Simon shook his head. "I thought a vacation might be a good idea."

"Not their idea of a vacation. It's a permanent one."

Simon grimaced. "Sorry, man. I didn't know. Believe me, I had no idea." He took a deep breath. "So Raven and this other girl resemble each other. Do you think there's any reason for that?"

"You mean are they related?" Beck scratched his chin. "They look enough alike to be twins."

All three men looked at Raven.

She shook her head. "My parents died when I was five. I don't have a twin, or even a sister. Sorry. Though I hate to think someone else went through what that man did to me."

Glancing at them all, her gaze finally settled on Simon. She remembered how he'd comforted her when she'd cried for that other little girl who'd had to deal with the professor.

"Since she disappeared," Simon said, holding her gaze, "I wonder if she went Fer—er, wild, like you."

Raven shrugged. Exhaustion washed over her and she stifled another yawn.

Zach finished his beer and glanced at his watch. "I'll let you guys finish catching up. I've got an early appointment in the morning, so good night." He squeezed Raven's shoulder. "You need to get some rest, too."

Meeting his gaze, she saw frank admiration, maybe even desire in his eyes. Though Zach was an attractive man, she felt…absolutely nothing. Not like the way Simon's gaze made her feel, all warm and boneless.

Interesting. Maybe even an epiphany of some sort, but she was so tired, too exhausted to try and figure that out now. Another yawn overtook her as she managed a weary smile. "That's the best idea I've heard since I came out here. Good night, you guys."

With an impersonal wave and a perfunctory smile, she turned and followed Zach out of the kitchen.

Turning the corner, she saw he waited for her outside the guest bedroom.

"Are you all right?" he asked.

Searching his face, she saw nothing but concern this time.

"I will be," she said. "As soon as I get some rest."

He didn't move, apparently not taking the hint. "I've known Simon since we were children," he said. "I've never seen him like this."

So tired she swayed on her feet, Raven peered up at him, trying to concentrate on his words. "Like what?"

As he searched her face, something he saw in her eyes appeared to satisfy him. His expression softened. "Never mind," he said softly. "Listen, I've got a motorcycle in the garage and a couple of spare helmets. I'll tell Simon, too. You guys are welcome to use it. Sleep well."

Watching him as he continued on down the hall to the room at the end, she waited until he'd closed his door before entering her room and doing the same.

She fell asleep almost as soon as her head hit the pillow.

Sometime in the night, Raven woke. Automatically reaching to touch the nearest wolf, she felt a deep sorrow as she remembered they were gone and she was alone, sleeping in a huge, plush bed in a strange house in a town she avoided like the plague. Still, she was clean and warm, safe and dry.

Then why was she so restless?

Simon. She wanted Simon.

Untangling herself from the covers, she swung her legs over the side.

Why hadn't he come to her? She thought she knew. Fear had kept him away. Fear. Something she'd become intimately familiar with.

Wide-awake now, she perched on the edge of her bed, recognizing the truth, a truth she hated.

She'd been living with fear for so long, she no longer fought against it. Now, tired of fighting, the time had come to confront her old enemy. This night, she'd battle fear and win.

Shaking her head at her own dramatic musings, she thought of the long, hard journey she'd taken to get this far. Yet even here, now poised on the brink of an entirely new chapter, she let fear control her life.

She wanted Simon. Desired him, with an intensity that sometimes frightened her. Assuming she made it through this mess, could she honestly live the rest of her life knowing she'd never acted on that desire? Could she live the rest of her life always wondering what making love with him would have been like, wondering if his touch could somehow erase the horrible, degrading acts that had come before?

She didn't think she could. Even if what she was now contemplating turned out to be a mistake, she wanted to know. Had to know.

She took a deep breath, again struggling against the fear. How did one act in a situation like this? She knew how a female wolf would act, but she was human now, right this moment, and had to go about this as a human woman would.

Telling herself that he wanted her as badly as she wanted him, she stood. Like her, Simon battled fear, fear of some ridiculous code of conduct, a rule that had been made by a corrupt organization. Were it not for that, she had no doubt he would have come to her long before now.

Thus fortified, she crossed the room. Moving

quietly, she opened her bedroom door. Glancing at the end of the hall to make sure Zach's door was still closed, she padded down the carpeted hallway in the opposite direction.

At the entrance to the living room, she stopped. Her breath caught in her throat. Moonlight spilled in the huge bay window at one end of the living room where Simon slept, illuminating him on the couch.

Moving closer, she watched him as he slept, her chest tight and her heart full of emotion. This man had become closer to her than anyone—her friend, companion and wolf-mate, all rolled into one. Now, if he was willing, they'd become lovers.

She swallowed hard and took a deep breath. Then, dropping the sheet she'd used to cover her nakedness, she reached for the corner of the blanket he slept under. Lifting one side, heart pounding, she slipped underneath, her slightly chilled body connecting with his warm one. She snuggled herself into position, spooning him from the front. Everywhere her skin touched his, she tingled.

And still, Simon slept.

He'd showered, too, and smelled of soap and

man. As her body warmed, he made a sound in his sleep, shifting himself to accommodate her. She pressed a tentative kiss at the hollow of his throat, then another, higher up, at the cleft of his chin, making him smile in his sleep.

To her surprise, he still didn't wake, his deep, even breathing a testament to the depths of his slumber.

Aroused and aching, she began her exploration, delighting in the feel of his muscular chest, skimming her fingers over his nipples until they pebbled and again tasting the skin on his neck.

Against her belly, his body swelled, lengthened and her body responded with a rush of warm wetness.

She knew when he woke. He stiffened. "Raven, what—"

Before he could protest, she kissed him, going on instinct, using her tongue to explore his mouth. His engorged body felt hot pressing against her, ready, his arousal intensifying her need.

He tried to resist her. As if by holding himself perfectly still he could will his desire away.

Like her, he knew once he gave in, there'd be no going back.

When he moved his head the moonlight caught

his face. The stark hunger she saw in his gaze made her mouth go dry.

Yet still he made no move to take things further.

Her body moving against him, she wondered if there were words to let him know what she wanted. Then, when he shuddered and gave a hoarse cry, she realized she wouldn't need words. His body understood and whatever inner war he waged, he was on the verge of losing.

"Raven, stop. You know this is wrong," he rasped. Against her chest, she could feel his heart pounding wild.

"No, it's right," she whispered, continuing to stroke his skin, her fingers playing over him, making him writhe in helpless need.

He opened his mouth, whether to protest or to speak, she didn't know. But, as she bent her head and began breathing tiny, nibbling kisses on his bare chest, he groaned instead.

"Raven, please…" As she took one of his nipples into her mouth, he gasped. He arched his back, his already aroused body pushing at her, telling her without words what she, unschooled in the ways of lovemaking, needed to do.

Lifting herself up until she was poised over

him, she slipped her body down, taking him deep into her. The fully aroused, hard length of him, all the way in, so tight she was surprised he fit.

Damn and double damn. She'd had no idea this act could feel so good.

The sensation felt so amazing, she couldn't keep from whimpering. Though she wasn't a virgin, her experience had only been limited to the professor and his repeated rapes. There'd been nothing of pleasure in those acts. Then, she'd known only shame and pain and loathing.

This…was nothing like that. Nothing at all. Experimentally, she moved, clenching him tight with her body. Ahh, no. She hadn't known such delight was possible.

Simon moved inside her. A moan escaped her, and she gripped his shoulders, moving with him, riding him, fierce and wild and strong.

He pushed harder, up, increasing the length and the depth of his penetration. She took all he could give her and more. No longer aware of the cold, nor of strange, human furnishings surrounding them, she gazed into Simon's eyes and saw… herself.

They were one, joined in more places than merely their bodies. If she had any sense, any sense at all, she'd get up and run away as fast as she could.

Except what they did together felt too damn good.

"How can you—" She gasped, arching her back, hot yet shivering, warming from the inside out. Her body throbbed, aching, aching, wanting, needing. More.

For an answer, he slanted his mouth over hers.

Kissing him, her world tilted. As his tongue matched the moves of their bodies, mating with hers, she plummeted over the edge.

Raven cried out into his mouth, tasting him, feeling him. Her body clenched around him, shuddering again and again and again. A second later, Simon ripped his mouth away from hers. "Raven," he cried, and found his own release.

They held each other while their heartbeats slowed. She couldn't stop touching him, his hair, his skin, his wonderful, sensual mouth. She wanted to cry, she wanted to laugh. Instead, she told him the truth. "I didn't know it could be like that."

Stroking her back, his own hand stilled. "It isn't normally, Raven."

She heard the worry in his voice. "Is that a bad

thing?" she asked, afraid to meet his gaze, afraid
of what she might see there.

"I don't know." He took a deep breath. "Look
at me."

Throat aching, she shook her head. Then, remembering her newfound oath to battle fear,
turned to meet his gaze.

The raw tenderness she saw in his face made
her suck in her breath.

"We have to talk about this." He kissed the
tip of her nose. "I never meant for this to
happen."

She couldn't help but chuckle. "I did." Lifting her
chin, she told him the truth. "And I'm glad it did."

"We didn't take precautions."

"Precautions?" She knew what he meant, but
some small part of her, already braced for hurt,
didn't want to understand.

"Birth control. You could get pregnant."

Pregnant. "Not your problem," she snapped.

"It *is* my problem. It takes two to make a
baby. If you have a child, that baby will be part
of me, too."

A baby. Even the word, echoing around inside
her head, opened up another raw spot inside.
Hugging herself, she bit her lip, unable to look at

him, aware her emotions were too raw, afraid she might—inexplicably—cry.

A baby. A baby. Family. Someone to love unconditionally. Hers.

And Simon's.

The next instant, she shook her head. Things like that didn't happen to people like her.

"You don't have to worry," she told him, some small, hurting part of her wanting to lash out and hurt him, too. "All the times the professor raped me, I didn't get pregnant. He didn't take precautions, either."

His expression darkened and a muscle moved in his jaw. "That man is lucky he's dead."

She started to move, to get up and return to her room.

"Wait," Simon told her. "Stay with me. Better yet," he kissed her again, "you've got a nice-size bed. Let's go back to it and get some sleep."

As they strolled toward her room, Simon promised himself if he touched her again, he'd make sure he had a condom.

The next morning, Simon woke to an armful of warm, curvy Raven. Remorse banished his contentment, remorse and fear that he'd crossed yet another threshold from which there was no going back.

He wondered when he'd begun turning into a man he didn't recognize.

He'd done the unthinkable. He'd slept with Raven, who, despite his growing dislike of the word, was a Feral. As a Protector, he'd been charged with protecting her, not exploiting her. Though according to Ross, he'd been charged with exterminating her.

His entire world had changed, and he wasn't entirely sure he wanted to go back to the life he'd had before. But then, he wasn't certain about anything.

Raven's amazing eyes opened. "Good morning." Smiling, she leaned toward him, her parted lips inviting his kiss.

Gritting his teeth, Simon bit back a groan, trying to figure out how to untangle himself without hurting her feelings. Despite his immediate arousal, what had happened earlier could not happen again. No protection.

"Don't," he growled.

She tore her gaze away from his face. "Don't what?"

"Don't look at me like you want to eat me up."

Her smile widened. "I'm sorry. I don't know what's wrong with me." Glancing at his aroused body, she licked her lips. "I'll try not to think about doing anything to you with my mouth."

He bit back a groan. If this line of talk kept up, his rapidly shredding resolve would be history.

Very aware of his arousal, she eyed him. "After all, most of my life, I've intentionally let my savage side have free rein. As humans, we've made love. Now my wolf wants to mate with yours. We're shifters, so I guess it's only natural, right?"

He couldn't speak. He needed a cold shower. Hell, he needed an ice pack. Something, anything, or he'd take her again right there, and…

Time to face the honest truth. Despite the intense lovemaking a few hours earlier, he craved Raven again.

He wondered if he'd ever get enough of her to slake this need.

Something of his thoughts must have shown on his face. Either that or she read his mind. "Come here," she said softly, opening her arms.

Still, he held himself back with the last shreds of his self-control. "Not without protection," he rasped. "I don't have any condoms."

"Oh." She bit her lip, managing to look completely sexy and innocent all at once. "Maybe Zach does? Why don't you ask him?"

"Zach said he was leaving early." He thought fast. "Let me check his bathroom."

Under Zach's sink, he found a small box of condoms, size extra large. Conscience fighting his desire, he took a couple and went back to the bedroom.

Where Raven waited, naked on the bed. "Did you find what you need?"

Struck wordless by the sight of her, he held up the foil packets, setting one on the nightstand.

"Then come here." She arched her back, giving him a clear view of the paradise that waited for him between her legs.

Somehow he got the condom open and worked it over his engorged arousal. Watching, Raven made sounds of encouragement, but didn't offer to help. From the look of puzzlement on her face, he thought she'd never seen a condom before. From the way his hand shook as he fumbled to get it on, one might think he hadn't, either.

Hellhounds, he wanted her. More than he'd ever wanted a woman and worse, he suspected after her, he'd never want another woman the same way again.

Did that mean she was his mate? Because that was highly unlikely and rare, he doubted it. Enough of this romantic nonsense. One thing life had taught him, when it came down to the nut cracking, only cold, hard facts mattered.

Fact—he wanted Raven. Whether or not she was his mate, well, right now, he didn't know, and as he pushed himself into her welcoming warmth, he told himself he didn't care.

Later, freshly showered, they sat in the kitchen and ate the fresh fruit and pastries Zach had so thoughtfully provided. He'd left a note stating he'd had an early appointment at a farm up in Berthoud and then would be working all day. They should use the house as their own and he'd see them later.

Simon's cell phone rang as he polished off his third pastry.

"You've got to get out of there," Beck said. "They grabbed Zach and are holding him for questioning. I'm trying to find out the status on him. But Ross knows you're there. I think he's got another team en route to take you out."

Stunned, Simon snapped the phone closed and

grabbed Raven's arm. "They grabbed Zach. Come on, we've got to get out of here."

She stared at him. "Zach? But why?"

"For questioning."

"Do they have jurisdiction over him?"

He shrugged. "He's not a shifter. He'll talk to him. But unless he's committed a crime, they'll have to let him go."

"Have to? Since when have those people ever played by the rules? How many people in your shifter pack know what this Society of Protectors does?"

She had a point. One he didn't like to think about.

"The important thing is that Zach's okay. But Beck said Ross has sent a team to pick us up. They know we're here. We've got to go."

Still she balked. "Go where? We don't have a car. Once we're outside on the sidewalk, we'll be open targets."

"Zach said we could use his motorcycle."

"Uh, no." She shook her head, sending her long braid flying. "There's no way I'm getting on that thing."

"We don't have a choice. We can't stay here. We'd be trapped inside this house." He took a deep breath. "How about... I know. There's a bus stop not too far from here. We can hop on the bus and go anywhere we want."

"One of these days, I'm going to have to stop running," she muttered. Grabbing her coat, she tossed him his. "You got your hat and gloves?"

"In my pockets." He pulled the hat onto his head, then put on the gloves. "Are you ready?"

She nodded. "As ready as I'm going to be."

Opening the front door, he checked the sidewalk in both directions. "It's clear. Come on."

They hurried up the sidewalk, turning left, heading up the hill. Their breath left white puffs of moisture in the frigid air.

"How far?" Raven kept glancing over her shoulder.

"Half a block." He pointed. "There."

About ten people huddled around a small wooden bench. "It's crowded, which I'll take as a good sign. That means the bus hasn't shown up yet."

"And it'll make it more difficult to spot us."

"Here comes the bus." They sprinted the remaining distance, arriving just as the bus lumbered to a stop. Climbing on board, he looked back at Zach's house. Still no sign of their pursuers.

"Now what?" Crossing her arms, Raven gave him a disgruntled look. "I wanted to check on Theo."

"We can't go anywhere near the clinic. They'll be watching for us."

After more muttering under her breath, she seemed to accept his words.

"What about Zach? How can we make sure he's okay?"

"Beck said he'd call me when he had news. And I'm sure Zach will text or something, once they let him go."

To his surprise, Simon realized the bus was heading north on the Diagonal Highway, toward Longmont. Just his luck to snag the bus that went completely out of town.

The first stop was at Twin Peaks mall on Hover Street, a small, older mall with a Dillard's on one end and a Sears on the other. Raven stared hard at the buildings, making him wonder if she'd ever seen a mall before. As soon as the doors opened, she jumped up and hurried off, leaving Simon no choice but to follow her.

He caught up with her as she barreled down the sidewalk toward the mall entrance. "Raven? What's up? Where are you going?"

"I saw her." She barely spared him a glance, yanking open the door. "She went into here."

"Who? Who did you see?"

Impatiently scanning the throngs of shoppers, she frowned. "The woman who looks exactly like me, though she appears much younger. The one your Society is desperately hunting."

Chapter 12

From the skeptical expression he wore, Raven knew Simon thought she'd lost her mind. But she knew what she'd seen. The instant she'd caught a glimpse of the younger other woman, she'd known she'd seen her doppelgänger.

Why here? But then again, why not? This aging mall would be the perfect place for them to hide from their pursuers, as well. Who would think of searching for them here?

Simon shook his head. "That would be too easy."

"Or too simple." She couldn't hide her grin.

"And if I'm wrong, and the girl I saw isn't the one, then we haven't lost anything. We can even grab a bite to eat."

"True." He glanced around, taking in the half-full parking lot. "But there will be a lot of people inside. How are you going to find one person, especially since you're not a hundred percent positive what you saw?"

"At least this isn't a large mall," she said, wondering at his unusual pessimism. "I saw what she was wearing. I really think we should be able to find her fairly easily."

To his credit, Simon didn't argue. "She could be anywhere," he warned. "I need a visual."

"She's younger than me, like maybe ten years. She's wearing jeans and a dark green, down jacket. Her hair is in a ponytail, but is the same as mine—color, curliness, everything."

"Good enough," he said and nodded. "Let's go."

"You go left, I'll go right." Raven kept looking, searching the crowded luggage store to her left, then the jewelry store to her right. "If you see her, stop her and talk to her. Keep her talking as long as you can and I'll find you."

"We're not splitting up. No way. We're staying together."

"Why?" Raven scoffed. "Do you think she's dangerous?"

"Of course not." Simon gave her a look full of long-suffering patience. "Don't forget you're not the only one looking for her. Just because you feel anonymous here doesn't mean we're safe. They're looking for her and for you. No way are we splitting up."

Put that way, he made sense. Raven took a second away from her frantic searching to glance at his familiar face.

"You're right," she told him. "Then come on, help me look. There aren't that many places to hide and the mall's not crowded at this time of the day. She's got to be here somewhere."

Agreeably, he ambled along beside her, checking out the stores on his side of the aisle. "What are you going to do once you find her?"

Surprised, she frowned up at him. "Talk to her, of course. She went through the same thing I did. Maybe she even knows why your Society wants us so badly."

Her choice of words seemed to bother him. "Quit calling them *my Society*. I'm not so sure I want to be affiliated with them any longer."

With difficulty, Raven hid her shock. Simon

didn't appear to realize the magnitude of his revelation. All along he'd been insisting his treatment by the Society was some sort of error. Now, he appeared to realize the truth—something was very wrong.

"Let's head toward the Sears store." Pointing, she started leading the way, checking into every small shop on her side. "Since she parked at this end, I'm going to assume she wanted one of these stores. We shouldn't have to walk very far to find her."

Half an hour later, after diligently scanning every small store, they stopped in front of the Sears.

"I'm beginning to think she didn't come here to shop." Raven couldn't keep the glumness from her voice. "She probably thought this would be a good place to lay low and while away some hours, like I did."

Simon didn't disagree. "Maybe we should return to the entrance where you first saw her. She'll eventually go out the same way."

"If she hasn't already left." Straightening her shoulders, Raven turned around and began trudging back the way they'd come. As they passed a long hallway with a sign pointing to the restrooms, she glanced down it, catching a glimpse of what looked like a green, down coat before the woman turned the corner.

"I think she's down there." Grabbing Simon's arm, she tugged, half pulling him down the hallway. Heart pounding, she kept herself to a brisk walk when in fact she wanted to run.

They turned the same corner, which dead-ended into a space with two restroom doors, one marked *Women* and the other marked *Men.*

"Wait for me," she said, pushing at the women's door.

"Hold on." Simon grabbed her back. "Take it easy. You've got to go slow, like you were approaching a wild wolf. The last thing you want to do is frighten her."

He talked as if Raven's look-alike might be Feral. Though she hated the word, she had to consider he might be right. "I'll be careful."

She pushed the door open. Inside the restroom, only one stall was occupied. Excellent. At least their first meeting would be in private. Arms crossed, feeling oddly defensive, Raven waited.

A moment later, the commode flushed and the stall door swung open. A young woman, a teenager really, emerged. The instant she saw

Raven, her gaze darted toward the doorway, as if she contemplating making a dash for it.

Why?

Raven stepped into her path. "Don't be frightened. I won't hurt you. I think you know who I am. Maybe we should talk."

"Go away," the woman said. "I didn't ask for you to bother me. Leave me alone."

That voice…uneasy now, Raven hesitated. It was her voice, inflections, accent and all. Facing a woman who could have been her younger mirror image, she didn't know how to act, what to say, what to do.

So she reiterated her plea. "Please, we need to talk. I can help you."

Lifting her lip in a grotesque parody of a wolf snarl, the woman shook her head. With her youth and inexperience, she couldn't hide her fear.

Like Simon had warned, she reminded Raven of a trapped wild wolf, desperate to flee.

Avoiding directly looking into her eyes since that was a sign of aggression to wolves, Raven lowered her head and took a small step forward. She pitched her voice low and soothing. "I mean no harm."

"Get back," the girl said, her voice changing

to a growl as she began yanking off clothing. An instant later, she changed. Her changing happened unbelievably fast, almost instantaneously. The change was unlike anything Raven had ever seen, though she knew she was relatively inexperienced. One moment the other woman stood there, human, fully clothed. The next, her clothing lay in a heap on the floor at the feet of a wolf.

A wolf with a coat the same midnight shade as Raven's beast.

While Raven stared in stunned shock, the wolf leaped for her.

Moving purely by instinct, Raven pivoted, just in time. The wolf crashed into the wall, still snarling as she slid to the floor.

Heart pounding, Raven knew she'd have to go into defensive mode. The shifter who looked enough like her to be her younger sister wanted to kill her!

Spinning around, Raven began her own transformation, pulling off her clothing and rushing it, even as the she-wolf picked herself up and shook off the effects of her crash against the wall.

One second. Two. Raven's change finished. Three seconds. She looked up. Four. The other sprang forward in another attack, this time wolf-to-wolf.

Baring her teeth, Raven met her halfway, ready. With her lupine blood surging and her heart pumping, she felt savagely glad she'd had the experience fighting wild wolves for her Alpha spot. Fighting she did well. Maybe with this girl it was only a matter of proving dominance. This, she could do.

She thought of her former foe, the she-wolf she'd called Mandy. Mandy had been larger, more aggressive in her fury. Fighting this teenaged shifter should be a piece of cake.

Raven scored the first point, a quick dash in, jaws locked on the other's flank. A tear, blood, a grunt of pain. Since she wasn't going in for the kill, Raven let go.

Piece of cake, huh? As they circled each other warily, Raven realized fighting this girl was different. This wolf seemed to know exactly how Raven would fight, how she'd move, when to dodge her lunges. This wolf met Raven's every parry with a countermove, yet managed to get in several teeth slashes, tearing open Raven's shoulder, then her chest.

The score, if one kept it, was now two to one.

Paws slipping on her own blood, Raven didn't know how this bitch did it, but she'd had enough. Though she normally used the human part of herself when fighting and hunting, now she did what she'd never done before, and let her wolf part take over completely, retreating to a dark corner of her own brain and shutting down human Raven.

Set loose, free, Raven's wolf attacked with a ferocious vengeance, slashing and snarling, spinning and ducking, using her teeth and her claws and the weight of her lupine body to chase the other, forcing her to back into a corner.

Not cowed, the other wolf crouched, baring her teeth, ready to fight to the death if need be.

Wolf-Raven rushed her, slamming her back into the ground, using teeth and claws to hold the other wolf down.

Victory! Standing over her, Raven prepared to rip out the other wolf's throat.

But something held her back. Her human half, struggling to regain dominance.

No. She could *not* kill this wolf.

Slowly, human Raven reeled her wolf-self back in, snarling and fighting all the way, eventually regaining control of her body, though she remained in her wolf shape, still standing over her conquest.

Believing death was imminent, the other wolf submitted. She shimmered once and changed back to human.

Still wolf, Raven snarled, baring her teeth.

To her credit, or stupidity, the Raven look-alike didn't cower. Instead, she lay still, her naked young body looking eerily familiar. Narrow-eyed, she waited for Raven to deliver the killing blow.

"Raven!" Simon's voice. The bathroom door swung open.

Never taking her attention from the captive woman, Wolf-Raven acknowledged his presence with one quick sweep of her tail.

He rushed over. "Let her go. What are you doing?"

Baring her teeth once more for good measure, Raven sighed and let go, backing off a step, then two.

The other girl kept still. Having already conceded to Raven, she didn't dare move.

Troubled, Raven began the change back to human. The instant she'd regained her form, she jumped to her feet and grabbed her clothes. Keeping an eye on the other, she hurriedly pulled on her pants, then her bra and shirt. When she'd finished dressing, she went to the floor, scooped up the other's discarded clothing and tossed it to her.

"Get dressed." The order sounded emotionless.

Face expressionless, the other woman complied, watching Raven through long, black lashes. Once she was fully clothed, she crossed her arms, her youthful expression mutinous.

"Who are you?" Raven asked. "How old are you? Where did you come from?"

No answer.

"Too many questions at once," Simon cautioned. "Ask one at a time."

Raven scowled. "I have no patience for this. She attacked me. I want answers. I want them now."

"Shh." Simon soothed, warning Raven with his gaze before looking at the girl. "Do you have a name?"

She glared at him, still silent.

Simon moved closer, his voice gentle. "We can help you if you let us."

"Help me?" she finally spat. "I don't need your help. I don't need anyone's help. I'm alone because I like to be alone. You people need to go away."

Raven read Simon's thoughts in his face. Feral. This woman was Feral, too.

As she had been. Finally, she understood why

they used this word. She, too, had been Feral. Once. Past tense. She wasn't anymore.

Stunned, she realized she had changed. She'd given her human side more importance than her wolf. She supposed this was some sort of progress.

Stranger still, she didn't mind at all. Tucking that revelation away to examine later, she focused on the young stranger.

"We're the same, you and I." Raven crossed her arms, too, mimicking the other's dismayed expression.

"No, we're not."

Raven lifted a lock of her black, curly hair. "Look in the mirror, sweetheart. Though you're younger, we look the same, move the same, even our wolves have similar coats."

"So?" She sounded bored.

Taking a deep breath, Raven went for broke. "You were caged by the professor, too, weren't you?"

The girl froze. "How do you know about that?"

"Because I was, too." Raven swallowed. "For years, before you. I finally escaped."

"You lie." The other narrowed her eyes. "He had only me. All my life. My earliest memories include him and him alone. I don't remember you. You weren't there."

"All your life? How is that possible?" Raven kept her arms crossed.

No reply. The two women glared at each other from identical brilliant blue eyes.

"Your entire life," Raven mused. "That's so odd…"

"How old are you?" Simon's clipped tone indicated the girl had better answer.

"Old enough," she shot back. "I'm over eighteen, if that's what you mean."

"You're what, nineteen?" Raven kept her voice gentle.

Sullen, the girl nodded.

"Do you have a name?"

"You can call me Cee. My real name is too ugly." She took a deep breath, then met Raven's gaze straight on. "Why did you lie to me about the professor?"

"I didn't lie. I was his prisoner for many years."

"Prisoner? Isn't that too strong of a word?"

Raven shrugged. "He kept me in a cage. What else would you call it?"

"He only put me in a cage once he realized I could change. He said he had to, for my own safety."

Outraged, Raven struggled to remain neutral but lost. "For your own safety? Have you ever attacked a human while you were wolf?"

"Of course not," Cee scoffed. "Why would I? I'd rather run and hunt and live my life. I don't need that kind of grief."

"Exactly. So tell me again why you had to live in a cage."

Rather than answering, Cee chose to focus on another technicality. "I didn't live there. He let me out to exercise and go to the bathroom."

Trying to hide her exasperation, Raven sighed. "Yeah? Me, too. But I slept there. I took my meals there. He kept me there like some wild animal in a zoo."

"Hmmph." Cee's scowl said plainly what she thought of that.

Raven had to ask the next question. "Did he ever...touch you?"

"Of course not." Bristling at the suggestion, Cee looked as though she wanted to attack.

"He did me," Raven said softly, sadly.

Her words deflected Cee's anger. "Why would he treat you like an animal and not me?"

"I don't know. Maybe he felt fatherly toward you, since he raised you from an infant?"

As Cee opened her mouth to speak, the bathroom door opened. A young mother with three small children in tow entered, stopping short when she saw Simon.

"What are you doing in the women's room?" she asked, her voice low and furious. "I'll give you three seconds to get out of here, and then I'm calling the police."

Brandishing a cell phone like a weapon, she shepherded her kids to the handicapped stall. "I mean it."

Cee covered her mouth with her hand, giggling.

"Sorry. We're just leaving." Simon took Cee by the arm, then hooked his other arm around Raven's. "Let's go."

Once outside, they stopped at the end of the long hallway as Cee dissolved into a fit of laughter.

Raven couldn't help but join in. Once she started, she couldn't seem to stop.

Simon leaned back against the wall, watching them, and waiting.

Finally, Raven wiped her eyes. "Are you hungry?" she asked Cee. "We could get lunch and talk?"

Wiping her eyes with an eerily identical gesture, Cee nodded. Looking in both directions, she glanced longingly at the Panda Express restaurant. "I could eat."

Simon linked arms with both of them and they made their way down the mall.

Once at the counter, they let Cee order whatever she wanted, which turned out to be six items. Raven ordered a meal, as did Simon. Once Simon paid, they each carried the loaded-down trays over to a secluded table where they had a good view of the doorway.

Cee reached for the food. While she scarfed down sweet-and-sour chicken as if she hadn't eaten in a week, Simon filled her in on the massive manhunt for them.

"I knew someone was looking for me," she said with her mouth full. "But I didn't know why. I figured they think I killed the professor."

Leaning forward, Simon waited until he had her full attention. "Did you?"

She didn't even stop chewing. "Of course not. Why would I?"

Raven had to clamp her mouth in a tight line to keep from commenting. She wanted to see what Simon would do.

Simon smiled pleasantly. "You didn't have a reason?"

Stuffing another fragrant piece of chicken in her mouth, Cee shook her head and continued chewing.

"The people that are looking for you have nothing to do with the police," he finally said. "I used to work for them. A man named Ross is running the manhunt for both you and for Raven."

"But why?" Cee looked from one to the other.

Still using his confidential tone, Simon shrugged. "Something the professor did is making Ross want you both pretty badly."

"Did?" Cee shook her head. "He didn't do much. Mostly, he was like my father."

That did it. "Like your father?" Raven exploded, pushing out of her chair. "How can you say such a thing? He put you in a *cage,* for goodness' sake. And if he treated you the same way he treated me, he did things no respectable father would do."

Cee barely even paused in her chewing. "Like what?" There was only a mild curiosity in her voice, as if she truly didn't know what Raven meant.

Raven sat back down with a thud. Face coloring, she found herself at a lack for words, staring at the teenager, hands clenched in her lap.

When Simon's hand closed around hers under the table, she stiffened.

"It's all right," he said. "Breathe."

So she did. In and out. In and out.

Watching them, Cee polished off the last of the sweet-and-sour chicken and started on the rice. Mouth full, she shook her head. "Are you going to explain or not?"

Explain. How did one explain to a true innocent about a monster?

"Do you have parents?" Raven asked. "Someone who taught you right from wrong?"

"Not that I know of." Finishing her rice in record time, the girl reached for the last egg roll. "Just the professor. Why?"

Cee was alone in the world, just as Raven had been. While she was sure that had significance beyond the professor not having to worry about nosy relatives, Raven couldn't figure out what.

Simon squeezed her hand. "Are you sure she's not your sister?"

Raven studied Cee, who continued to eat and watch them with interest. "Positive. Though we look identical, if she's nineteen, I was ten when she was born. My parents had been dead five years by then."

"As far as you know."

"Oh, I know," she said grimly. "I attended their funeral."

"You were only five."

"I still remember bits and pieces." And the gut-wrenching feeling that her world had been turned completely upside down.

"Was it an open casket?"

"I don't remem—" She bit her lip. "I don't think you want to go there." Delivering the warning in a soft voice, she leaned forward. "If you're trying to say my parents are still alive, stop right now. There's no way they could have been alive and left me. I was made a ward of the state. They loved me. I know. They would have come for me."

Though he nodded, he didn't look convinced. "Fine. Back to my original statement. Something the professor did to you both has to be the reason Ross is pulling out all the stops to find you."

She shook her head, more than willing to get back on track. "He did horrible things to us and they want to punish us for that? Their priorities are screwed up."

Simon looked from Raven to Cee, his expression thoughtful. "What about experiments? Any implants of any kind? Drugs? Tests?"

Pushing away her now-empty tray, Cee leaned back in her chair, a contented look on her young face. "That was good. Thanks."

"You're welcome. Cee, did the professor do any tests on you?"

"Of course he did." Again she sounded supremely unconcerned. "He was always testing for something. That was his way of showing he cared."

"What a bunch of—" Raven had to bite back the words.

"Crap?" Cee finished for her. "Maybe to you, but he really cared about me. He said ones like me usually don't live long and he wanted to make certain I did."

"Ones like you?" Both Simon and Raven pounced on the words. "What did he mean?"

"I dunno." She gave them a smile so exactly like Raven's it was eerie. "I always took it to mean he thought I was special."

Raven wanted to curse. This was getting them exactly nowhere. "Where do you live, Cee?"

Still supremely unconcerned, Cee grinned. "Wherever I can find a place to crash. I was staying at my house, but ever since the professor died, I've been moving around. One thing he taught me was to avoid the police. As soon as they showed up, I peaced out."

"Peaced out?"

"Left." Her grin widened. "I've snuck back in there twice since, to get my backpack and clothes. Since he homeschooled me, I don't have any friends, so I've pretty much been on my own."

"That's where being able to change into a wolf comes in handy," Raven muttered.

"I was just about to say that." Openmouthed, Cee stared. "How did you know?"

"Because that's what I did. I've been living up in the mountains, staying wolf as long as I could. It's a lot warmer, isn't it?"

"And easier, too, most of the time." Cee's grin faded. "But didn't you get lonely?"

Inexplicably, staring at the younger girl's forlorn expression, Raven's throat began to ache. "I didn't think I did," she said slowly, squeezing Simon's hand. "But now I realize I must have been. Though I always had my wolves for company."

"Wolves? Awesome." Cee stood, wiping her hands down the front of her blue jeans. "Well, thanks for the food and everything, but I've got to go. The professor said if anything like this happened, I should always keep moving."

Though she had to clench her teeth at the way the teenager kept quoting the professor as if he were a god, Raven couldn't help but wonder out loud at Cee's words. "If anything like what happened?"

Shifting her weight from one dirty tennis shoe to the other, Cee shrugged. "You know, like this? Where people are looking for me. He told me they might, someday."

Raven struggled to contain her excitement. Now maybe they could finally get somewhere. "Did he tell you why?"

"Nope." Lifting her hand in a casual wave, Cee turned to leave. "I'm going to peace out now."

"Wait." Raven started to grab her arm, then thought better of it. "You can't go. I mean, we're sort of in this together."

Rocking back on her heels, Cee frowned with impatience. "No, we're not. I don't even know you."

"Look," Simon stepped in, his voice smooth and reasonable. "The same people are after you both. We should stick together."

"Why? If we're together and they find one, they've got us both. No way." She started to walk off and got about three paces away before she stopped and turned. "Hey, do either of you have a cell phone?"

Simon nodded.

"Let me see it." Cee held out her hand.

Showing no reluctance, Simon fished the phone out of his pocket and handed it over. Cee punched in some numbers and handed it back. "Now you've got my number. Call me later so I can store yours. I'll be in touch." And she sauntered off, looking like she hadn't a care in the world.

Raven turned to Simon. "We can't just let her go."

"We don't have a choice," he said, dragging his hand across his jaw. "And what she said does make partial sense. For whatever reason, they want both of you. Why make it easier for them by having you both in the same place?"

"But she's only nineteen."

"And an adult. Come on." He took her arm. "Let's get on another bus and find a motel. I've got some cash. We need to get a room and figure out what we're going to do."

The exit door was only fifty feet away when Simon saw them. Two men, wearing military fatigues and dark sunglasses.

"Protectors," Simon said softly. "Pretend a sudden interest in looking at costume jewelry."

Casually, Raven turned into the store on her

right, staring intently at a display of dangly earrings.

Gradually, she moved toward the back of the store, putting a large, center-aisle display between herself and the door. A moment later, Simon joined her.

They both jumped at a loud crash from farther down the aisle.

Out in the main part of the mall, someone screamed.

Chapter 13

Though his first impulse was to dash out into the aisle, Simon grabbed Raven's arm instead. "Stay put," he whispered. "I think it's a trick to flush us out."

She shifted her weight from one foot to the other, her expression anguished. "But what if that was Cee? What if those two guys in camo grabbed her?"

His gut clenched. Though he really didn't know the teenager, she looked so much like Raven he felt like they were old friends. "I'm pretty sure she left."

"But you're not sure. That sounded like a teenager."

"It might have been a couple of kids, horsing around."

"No." She shook her head. "It's not even three o'clock. I think most kids are still in school. It could have been Cee. We've got to help her."

The salesclerk, a twentysomething, multi-pierced person of undetermined gender, wandered over. "Can I help you find something?" From the voice, he was a male. He hadn't even reacted to the scream, which made Simon think such things were pretty common occurrences.

"No, thanks." Raven flashed him a fake smile. "We were just looking."

The kid nodded and turned to go.

"Wait." Simon decided to ask. "Did you hear that sound a minute ago? It sort of sounded like a scream."

"Yeah." The guy grimaced. "Someone's always yelling out there and stuff. Lots of teenagers come here and hang out." He said the word *teenagers* with scorn, apparently to prove he was older. "Screams are pretty commonplace. I've gotten to where I just ignore them."

Raven grimaced. "What if it was serious?"

"It wasn't. Believe me."

"Oh." Simon kept his expression bland. "Thanks."

"Yeah. Well, if you don't need anything..." The clerk glanced at his watch, as though he had something important to do. When neither Simon nor Raven contradicted him, he wandered off to another part of the store.

"That still could have been Cee," Raven said, the second he was out of earshot. "We won't know unless we go and find out."

"There's no sense endangering you for a remote possibility."

"Those two men might have grabbed Cee." But now even Raven didn't sound certain.

"If they did, there's nothing we can do." He held up a hand. "Right now. First, those guys are armed, I'd bet you anything. The last thing we want them to do is start shooting in a public mall."

"Surely they wouldn't do that?" Raven looked shocked. "Too many innocent people would get hurt."

"Somehow, I don't think they would care." The new breed of Protectors, if they even still called themselves that, appeared to hold to an entirely different set of ethics than the ones Simon knew by heart.

"How dare they even call themselves Protectors," Raven said. Simon stared, startled that her words exactly mirrored his thoughts.

"What? What's wrong?"

He shook his head. "Nothing." He listened, head cocked, then nodded. "Okay, I don't hear any more screams. Let's slowly walk out of this store. We're going to head toward the exit."

"But Cee—"

"I've got her number. I'll call her later, once we're out of this place."

"Simon…"

"Listen to me." He took her arm. "Do you want to go out there and announce your presence to those guys?"

"I—" She bit her lip.

"Then do as I ask." At the stricken look on her beautiful face, he attempted to soften his tone. "Please. Cee probably left right before we did. Give the girl some credit. She's smart. She's been able to avoid them this long."

Finally, Raven took a deep breath. "You know what? I'm tired of running." She gave him a look full of defiance. "If they want me, I'm going to let them have me."

His heart stopped dead in his chest. "Absolutely not. Eventually they've got to—"

"No." Though her interruption sounded harsh, her smile wavered toward a kind of frightened bravery. "You've tried enough times to make them see reason. They've demonstrated over and over that they won't. It's time to move on to plan B."

"Plan B. I don't have a plan B." He thought furiously, hoping they could settle on some sort of compromise. "Let's talk about this more later. We can hash out something. You know we've got to work out a few more details."

"No, we don't. We're going with my plan B."

"What, committing suicide? That's your plan? After all we've done trying to keep you alive?"

"Giving myself up wouldn't necessarily mean they'd kill me."

He cursed, low and furious. "Haven't you learned anything in the time we've been together?"

Lifting her chin, she nodded. "I've learned a lot. And I don't think we're ever going to get any answers if we keep running."

"Answers? Do you really think they're going to tell you anything?"

"They might, if we go about this the right way. I told you, I've got a plan."

Every second that he could keep her talking bought them time. The longer he could prevent her from doing anything drastic, the more chance the Protectors had left the mall.

"You've got a plan?" He spoke in a way to let her know he was only humoring her, knowing provoking her would make her more inclined to argue and discuss, rather than simply act. "And your plan would be?"

"I'm taking the battle public." She glanced past him into the mall. "I'll go out there and make a scene. They won't dare to murder me in front of the entire world."

"You never know." He knew he spoke the truth, sadly. "This new breed of Protector seems to care about nothing but getting the job done."

"Then I'll go to the media. Tell my story. They'll put me on the news. I would think such a thing would make headlines around the word, especially if I let them film me changing."

If he'd thought she couldn't shock him more, he'd been wrong. "Let them film you... Raven, you can't. Sometimes I forget you led a sheltered life. The entire human part of the world doesn't know about shape-shifters."

Again she tilted her chin up at him in that stubborn way he was coming to know. "Maybe it's time they found out."

"No, it's not." He sighed. "You don't know about this, because you weren't given a proper shifter education, but that particular argument has been going on for years. Several people have tried over the centuries. Never a good thing."

"Times have changed. People are more accepting. What is the worst that could happen? We'd be ostracized?"

At least this discussion was helping him stall for time.

"No, much worse than that. Mankind would panic. Suspicion would give way to hysteria, lynch mob mentality. The pack would be slaughtered."

"Surely not. What with the discrimination laws in place now and all—"

"Those laws were made for humans. Not monsters."

She hissed at his choice of word. "We're not monsters."

"Yeah? Try telling that to a panic-stricken mother who believes the big, bad werewolf is going to eat her baby. They've always thought us monstrous. That's one thing that's never going to change."

Finally, Raven seemed at a loss for words. At least, she appeared to be mulling her decision over. Simon hoped she would reconsider. Just in case she didn't, he needed to come up with a better plan. Something to distract her. Something that might actually work. But what?

A group of giggling teenage girls entered the store, glancing curiously at them before dismissing them as a couple of unhip old people. Still holding Raven's arm, Simon stepped aside to let them pass, wondering if one of them had been the one who'd screamed earlier.

He sure as hell hoped so. He didn't want to think about what it would mean if the Protectors had been successful in grabbing Cee.

"Please reconsider," he said once they were alone again. "There's got to be another way."

"I think you're overreacting." Her smile told him she meant to try her plan, no matter what he claimed.

Which meant he'd have to stop her. But how?

While he puzzled that one out, Raven shook off his arm and stepped out into the mall. Simon hurried to catch her.

"What are you going to do, start screaming?"

For the first time, a look of uncertainty crossed her face. "I just figured I'd make myself noticeable. If they're still here, they'll see me. After that, it's their move."

"And if they shoot you?" His gut knotted at the thought of that. "What do you want me to do then, leave you here to die?" As if he would, as if he could.

"They won't shoot me." She sounded confident. "The head-honcho guy, your boss—"

"Ross."

"Yes, Ross. He wants something from me. And from Cee. I think he needs us alive."

"Beck says the order is kill on sight. Dead or alive. I told you that."

"You did. But what does Beck know, really? He's on the run from them, too. He's not exactly in the loop, now, is he?"

Put that way, Simon had to admit she had a point. "For now, can we get out of sight for a minute?" He pulled her over to a makeup store, half dragging her toward the sale shelves located in the back.

"Why?"

"Let me call Cee," he said, still trying to stall and keep her from doing anything foolish. "If

she's free, will you at least wait a little longer
before giving yourself up?"

Though she hesitated, finally she nodded.
"Okay. Call her."

Scrolling through the address book, he located
Cee's entry and hit Send. But instead of answering, the call went to her voice mail.

Watching Raven, who pretended to be engrossed in a display of mineral makeup, he left a
terse message explaining the situation and hung
up after asking Cee to call him immediately. He
muttered a quick prayer under his breath that she
hadn't been captured. "I got her voice mail."

"I know, I heard. But why did you say I was
suicidal?" Raven asked. "I'm not trying to kill
myself."

About to answer, his trepidation gave way to
triumph as his phone rang. "Thank the hounds,"
he said as Cee's name showed up on the display
screen. Answering, he couldn't help but relay his
worries to the teenager.

"No, they didn't get me," she said in response
to his query. "I saw those two goons come in, so I
hightailed it out of there. I'm clear across town,
though I was worried about you guys. Why does
Raven want to commit suicide? Something I said?"

He had to chuckle at the teenager's dry tone. "Ask her yourself."

"Put her on," Cee demanded. "I want to talk some sense into her."

"Okay." He handed Raven the phone. "Cee wants to talk to you."

Listening while Raven spoke to Cee, he didn't bother to hide his smile. Judging from Raven's end of the conversation, the girl ripped Raven a new one.

"Okay, okay. I'll call you later," Raven promised, then closed the phone. She gave Simon a chagrined grimace. "She made me feel like an idiot."

"I hate to agree with her, but you were." Putting his arm around her shoulders, he gave her a quick hug to soften the blow. "Those field guys are following orders. They won't listen to reason."

"Then who would?"

He took his time answering. "I don't know. That's why I'm having so much trouble coming up with a plan. I don't know who's normal and who's not. I used to think Ross—"

"That's it! Simon, I know what we can do!" Raven jumped up and down twice, barely able to contain her excitement. "You know how I said I was tired of running?"

"Yes," he answered cautiously, almost afraid to hear what she'd say next.

"I still am. But okay, I have to admit maybe my idea about letting them get me here in the mall wasn't a good one."

"I'll say." He glanced at the doorway, relieved to see no sign of the two Protectors.

"But I have another idea. A much better one." She took a deep breath. "Simon, you know where the Protector's headquarters is, right?"

"Of course I do. I worked at headquarters."

Grinning, she watched him closely. "Then let's go there, right now. If we show up unannounced, I'll bet we can confront this Ross, face-to-face."

Go there. At first, he wanted to dismiss her plan instantly. But the more he thought about it, the more he believed it just might work.

"They'll certainly never expect that," he said slowly. "If we time it properly, we can get inside and catch Ross alone and unprotected."

"Perfect." She crossed her arms. "And if we have to, we can even use him as a hostage."

"Good plan." He gave her an admiring glance. "Sometimes I find it hard to believe you lived isolated up in the mountains with a pack of wild wolves."

She laughed. "I told you, I read a lot. I've even been known to catch a movie now and then, when I was in town."

Hounds, she made him want to… He kissed her then, right there in a store full of women, unable to resist. "You're amazing, you know that?"

"No." Though she batted her eyelashes at him in false modesty, he could tell his words pleased her. "Let's get out of here."

One more hug and he let her go. Instantly, he got serious. "Will you do what I say?"

She didn't even hesitate. "Of course." Then, flashing him a quick grin, she amended her statement. "This time."

"Good enough. Now walk slowly, as if you don't have a care in the world."

"One, two, three, go."

They strolled back out into the mall aisle. The crowds had grown in size, mostly teens and preteens, maybe because school had let out now. As they passed a woman's clothing store, Simon spied a woman's brightly striped ski cap and got an idea.

"Wait." Snatching the cap off the mannequin,

he went to the counter and paid for it. Returning to Raven, he handed her the bag. "Put this on."

"Why? I'm not cold."

"No, but you need to hide your hair. There aren't too many women with hair like yours."

She frowned, apparently puzzled. "I have long, curly hair. Lots of women do."

"But not that particular inky shade of yours. You have beautiful hair, Raven, but you need to hide it for now."

Removing the hat from the sack, she pulled it over her head, tucking her long braid up into it. "There. Does that look better?"

He adjusted one wayward lock and nodded. "Perfect. Let's go."

They reached the door without incident and stepped outside into the gray, wintry day.

Raven squinted at the change in light. "So, tell me about this Protector headquarters. How long does it take to get there?"

He kept his hand lightly on her arm. "For this region, it's not too far. A couple of hours, driving. It's located down in The Springs."

"The Springs?" She nudged Simon's side. "Where's that?"

Hellhounds. As his body stirred, he shook his

head, realizing that, in all the excitement, he'd forgotten to purchase protection. He made a mental note to stop at the first drugstore he found and do exactly that.

"Colorado Springs," he told her. "Come on."

They reached the bus stop, watching as the big white bus lumbered to a stop on the other side of the mall. Just a few more minutes and they'd be safe. Simon normally wasn't a betting man, he'd always left that to Beck, but the odds looked good that they'd somehow managed to evade the best trackers in the shifter world.

Once they were home free, he'd take the time to wonder about that, but for now, he was simply counting his blessings.

"Here comes the bus," he muttered. "You get on first. Scope out the other passengers, but whatever you do, don't react no matter who you see."

She bit her lip. "Do you think they might be on here? I'd think they have their own transportation."

"They probably do, but you never know. Protectors are very thorough." Odd, the more he talked about his former occupation, the more he felt as if he was simply reciting dogma rather than stating facts. Another development he'd examine more closely later.

"Get seats as close to the front as you can."

"Easy on, easy off. Okay." She nodded. "You know, even though Colorado Springs isn't all that far, we don't even have a car. How are we going to get there?"

The bus moved toward them, way too slowly for Simon's peace of mind.

"Beck does." He tapped on his cell. "Once we're out of here, I'll call him and see if he'll let us borrow it." He didn't want anything to tie up his hands or his concentration until he knew they were in the clear.

"Don't talk about our plans anymore," he warned. "Talk about completely ordinary stuff, like the weather."

Adrenaline pumping, he took Raven's arm as the bus pulled up and stopped.

Following her, he got on and did a quick scan of the other passengers.

Though he saw one other shifter, there were no Protectors on board.

Relief flooded him as they took their seats. The second row was completely empty. Raven took one aisle seat to the left, he took the other on the right.

"Where do you want to go now?"

"Back to Boulder. Once we're there, I'll give Beck a call. I'd like to check on Zach, too."

"And Theo," she pointed out, sounding concerned. "I need to see how he's doing, if he made it through the night."

The drive back to Boulder seemed to take forever. They made a couple more stops and each time a passenger got on, Simon tensed.

When they rolled to a stop on Twenty-eighth Street, he stood up to get off and indicated to Raven that she should precede him.

"Call Beck," she urged as they watched the bus pull away. "See if he'll loan us his car."

"I'm not going to tell him what we're planning to do. If I did, he'd want to go."

"Maybe he should come," Raven said. "We can use all the help we can get."

Part of him thought she might be right. The other part, the body part he didn't normally use in place of his brain, protested. "Beck's kind of unpredictable right now."

"So are we," she pointed out. "If they're really chasing him like he says, then he has a right to confront them, too. We can make our own small army."

In theory, he liked the idea. Except three didn't

an army make. "Even if we could get Zach to come, four isn't enough to take on Ross and all his guys. I think it would be better if we went alone."

"I know." She held up her hand to stop him from saying anything else. "Less chance of being noticed."

He punched in Beck's number. The phone rang and rang, making Simon think he might get voice mail. But on the fifth ring, someone answered. Only the voice didn't belong to Beck.

"Is that you, Caldwell?" Ross. "Since caller ID shows *Whearly* and you have his phone, I'm guessing it is. Are you wanting to speak to your friend Beck here?"

Clenching the phone, Simon had to fight to keep the fury from his voice. "Where is he? What have you done?"

Ross laughed. "Beck is back within the protective folds of the Society. Nice and safe, and where we can look after him and make him better."

"How did you find him?"

"You know us. We have ways."

"Satellites, you mean."

"Hey, it's not my fault if you guys don't

remember that cell phones can act like a GPS. Dumb and dumber, I think."

Simon let that one go. Right now, Ross had all the cards. "What do you want, Ross?"

"I want the same thing I've always wanted. The Feral. Actually, both of them. I've dispatched teams to bring yours and the other one in."

"I know. I saw them today," Simon mocked. "They're losing their touch, Ross. They were within fifty feet of her, but didn't even notice."

"Oh, yeah?" Ross sounded supremely unconcerned, which Simon suspected was an act. "Well, let me throw another wrench in your plans. I've got your friend the vet, and now Beck. I'll trade you, my two for yours."

"Mine? I've only got one."

"Yeah, but you were the best Protector I had, Simon. If anyone can round up the other girl, you can. Have them at Folsom Field at sunrise in two days' time. The weather report is predicting more snow, which is a good thing for us."

"And if I don't? What if I can't find the other girl?"

Ross laughed. "You will. I have no doubt about that. Be there at sunrise. Otherwise, you'll never get a chance to tell your friends goodbye."

Letting the other man think he would do as he was told would provide the perfect cover.

"Will you be there?" Simon asked. "I'd like to turn them over to you personally."

"Of course not." Ross laughed again, the sound sending a chill down Simon's spine. "You know I'm too busy to get involved in fieldwork. But I'll be there in spirit. Oh, and tell your Feral lady friend," Ross added, almost as an afterthought, "I also have her pet wolf. The animal's still unconscious, though that will change if I stop the pain meds. Tell her if she turns herself in, I'll make sure the wolf is cared for. If not, the animal will suffer, I promise you."

"You son of a bitch," Simon choked out. "That's an innocent animal."

"Yeah, we all are." Again, Ross chuckled. "We all are sons of bitches. Caldwell, you have two days." With that final warning, Ross hung up.

Two days. Not much time. They'd have to make it work.

"What happened?" Raven clutched his arm. "What happened to Beck?"

As quickly as possible, he told her, skimming over most of Ross's threats about Theo, though he refused to outright lie.

"If he touches one hair on that young wolf's head, I'll kill him with my own hands," she swore.

Since he'd been thinking exactly the same thing, Simon didn't disagree. He wondered if he was getting used to the odd way they seemed to echo each other's thoughts.

"What now?" She asked, her expression haunted. "Are we going to meet them? At least the two days buys us a little time."

"Not likely. First off, that's exactly what Ross wants you to think. He's not going to call off his Protectors and sit back and wait for us to show up. And second, I sure as hell am not going to get you and Cee, and hand you over at Folsom Field. I like your idea. We're going to headquarters and confront Ross."

"We still don't have a car."

"True, since Beck is out of commission and can't lend us his, we're going to borrow Zach's motorcycle. Remember, he said we could use it." Reaching into his pocket, he pulled out the key.

"The motorcycle," she said faintly.

He waited for her to protest further. When she didn't, he continued, "We've got to haul ass to Texas. I want to get there before we're supposed to meet them at Folsom Field. The last thing Ross will expect is for us to show up on his doorstep."

Finally she nodded. "We've just got to get the motorcycle out of Zach's garage without getting caught. How are you going to do that? I'm pretty sure they'll be watching the house."

Taking her arm, he steered her in the direction they needed to go. "Let's start walking. We can figure out something on the way."

Chapter 14

They reached Zach's street as dusk was settling over Boulder. The first flakes of yet another snowstorm drifted down.

Spotting the house, they both stopped dead. There was a van parked in Zach's driveway.

"Zach doesn't own a van," Simon said. "We're going to have to go in the back way. I'm pretty sure his gate's unlocked."

"What about the dogs?"

He squeezed her shoulder. "You're not afraid of them anymore, are you?"

"No, but I hope they're all right."

Simon's stomach twisted. "Hopefully Ross's guys wouldn't have any reason to hurt them. They probably just put them out in the backyard."

"If they're there, won't they bark when we try to sneak in? That will alert whoever's in Zach's house."

He gave her a considering glance. "Not if we do this right. Come on."

They went around the block, coming in from the opposite direction. On the western corner of his property, Zach had two huge spruce trees.

"Stay behind these," Simon warned. "Just in case someone is looking out the window."

As he'd thought, the wooden gate was unlocked. They entered the backyard, which, because of the slope of the land, was level with the top floor of the house. From the covered patio, steps led down to a back door, which entered the den.

"See that window?" Simon pointed to the left of the patio. "The garage is there. We've got to cross the back of the house without them seeing us and squeeze through that."

Raven gave him a doubtful look. "I'm sure I can get through there, but you?"

"I can do it." He spoke with more confidence

than he felt. "The trick will be to do it undetected. Are you ready?"

She nodded.

"One, two, three, go."

They dashed across the yard, keeping as close to the house as possible. Once they reached the window, they both stood motionless, eyeing each other through the snowflakes.

"No dogs barked," she fretted. "I hope they're okay."

"I'm sure they're fine." He hoped they were. "Zach would go ballistic if anyone hurt his beloved dogs."

With much tugging, he managed to open the garage window.

"How come it's not locked?"

"I guess because it leads into the garage. Or maybe because this is Boulder. The natives here are pretty laid-back about stuff like that." Stepping aside, he gestured for her to precede him. "Ladies first."

Feet first, Raven wiggled on her behind until halfway in. Then she turned, gripping the windowsill, and went inside. He heard the quiet thud of her feet as she dropped to the ground.

His turn. Fitting his larger frame inside would be much more difficult, but doable.

After much scraping and grunting, he finally made it. Dropping to the floor, he turned to find Raven eyeing the motorcycle. In the dim light, the black bike looked more like a beast and less like a machine.

"What *is* that thing?" Raven whispered. "I mean, I know it's a motorcycle, but I've never seen anything like it before."

"Hellhounds." Circling the bike, Simon couldn't contain his awe. "That's a Ducati 900 Supersport. When Zach mentioned he had a motorcycle, I had no idea. This thing must be his pride and joy. I'm surprised he'd even offer to let us borrow it."

From the house, they heard a dog barking. Someone shouted at the animal to be quiet.

"We've got to get out of here." Simon grabbed a helmet from the metal shelves on the back of the garage. "Put this on."

Grimacing, she did as he asked, fastening the strap under her chin while he did the same with the other helmet. "Are you sure you can ride this thing in the snow?"

He hadn't driven a motorcycle in years, not since he and a friend had gone dirt biking as teens. Of course, he didn't tell her that. Instead, he told her the truth. "It won't be easy, but we don't have a choice."

"What about the keys?"

Simon pulled them out of his pocket. "Right here. The trick is going to be getting the garage door up and taking off without them shooting at us." He gave her what he hoped was a reassuring smile. "Are you ready?"

Gaze never leaving his face, she slowly nodded.

"We're going to crouch low, so hold on to me, okay?"

"Less of a target?"

He grinned. "That, and it'll give us more speed. Let's hope it starts."

Punching the garage-door opener, he jumped on the bike, depressed the hand clutch and turned the key.

The engine roared to life.

"Thank the hounds." He gunned the engine. As soon as the garage door, which moved far too slowly, made it halfway up, they shot forward.

Three men, ran out of the house and into the garage. One came out of the front of the house. He had a gun.

Simon turned east as he drove the motorcycle out of the garage. If the guy squeezed off a shot or two, he missed them. They roared off into the snowfall and the rapidly approaching night.

Knowing Twenty-eighth Street would turn into US 36, Simon lucked into every streetlight. If the bad guys got into their van meaning to follow them, Simon saw no signs. Maybe they honestly believed he'd meet them at Folsom Field in two days, with both Raven and Cee in tow.

Glad of their warm ski jackets and gloves, despite the helmet shield, Simon's chin soon felt frozen. He hunched into his coat, snuggling under the collar, which felt somewhat better. Behind him, Raven tucked her face into his back, hopefully keeping warm that way. As they roared onto the toll road to get them through Denver, the snow tapered off, then stopped.

On I-25, they stopped in Castle Rock for coffee and warmth. Though Raven's nose looked red, she seemed none the worse for wear. And, Simon thought, cute as hell. Limiting himself to a quick kiss on the cheek, he drank his coffee.

"What time does the office open?" Raven asked, watching him over her cup. "And where are we going to spend the night?"

"We'll get a motel," he told her. "There are several right there on the interstate once we get into town."

She nodded. "That way we can get a good night's rest."

But the image that came to mind when he thought of a hotel room involved tangled sheets and Raven naked beneath him. He swore under his breath, belatedly remembering he'd meant to get condoms.

Her slow smile told him she'd read his mind.

"Sometimes I think I can hear your thoughts in my head." With a groan, he dragged his fingers through his shaggy hair. "That shouldn't be possible, can't be possible. Unless…"

"Unless what?"

"Never mind. We need to sleep," he told her, his heartbeat speeding up at her wicked smile. "Nothing more."

She nodded. "You're right, of course." Standing, she walked gracefully over to the trash can and dropped her cup in. Simon couldn't take his eyes off her and, despite his still-chilled state, his body stirred.

She had the damndest effect on him. And he realized as long as he could be around her, he didn't want to ever feel normal again.

Draining the last of his coffee, he stood and followed her outside into the cold night.

The sky started spitting snow as they neared the city limits. Pulling into the parking lot of the first motel they saw, Simon left Raven with the bike. He went into the office, paid cash and got a key to a room with two double beds.

Rejoining her, he pointed to a door midway down the building. "We can walk. I'm bringing the motorcycle inside. Zach would never forgive me if someone stole this thing."

After he unlocked the door, she helped him brush off the snow and wheel the bike in.

"What about the carpet? Should we put a towel under the tires?"

"No." He pointed at the ancient green shag. "Nothing could make that rug any worse. Don't worry about it."

Once the door had been locked and the chain pulled, he pointed to the double beds. "We each can have our own."

Raven nodded. Avoiding eye contact, she strolled around the small room, turning on every light. Finally, she turned and faced him, her beautiful face a perfect mask. "Two beds? Why? I thought we could…"

He swallowed. "I'm not going to pretend I don't want you, because you know I do, though you have no idea how badly."

"Then why?"

The vulnerability in her eyes made him ache to take her in his arms. But he knew he couldn't touch her, so he kept his hands at his sides. "Raven, I didn't have time to get protection. We can't take that chance."

Her sudden smile lit up the room. She reached into her jeans pocket and pulled out a packet. "Remember that second condom you put on the nightstand? I didn't want to leave it there for Zach to see, so I stuck it in my pocket."

Struck speechless, he still couldn't move.

She sashayed over to him. "Let's put this thing to good use, shall we?"

The next morning Raven woke, sated and pleasantly sore. When she opened her eyes, she realized the bed was empty. The sound of the shower told her Simon had gotten up before her.

Knowing he'd wake her, she snuggled into the covers and tried to drift back off to sleep. But though her tired body could use more rest, there was too much at stake this day. Finally, she abandoned the attempt and sat up, using her pillow as a bolster. Clicking on the television, she saw the top news story was an out-of-control fire at the University of Colorado in Boulder. Her heart caught as she recognized the blazing building. She ought to, as she'd spent several years of her life caged there. The professor's laboratory was an inferno.

Simon emerged from the bathroom just as the program cut to a commercial. She filled him in and both watched silently as the news program came back on.

"A total loss," the announcer said. "Firefight ers are trying to keep the flames from spreading to any other buildings. We'll keep you updated as developments occur."

Raven switched off the TV. "I wonder if Ross had something to do with this?"

Pacing, Simon nodded. "I think he did. I've been trying to understand his rabid interest in the professor and the shifters he'd tortured. It has to have something to do with the professor's experiments."

"Now that the lab is gone, any evidence of whatever the professor was working on will be destroyed."

"Unless Ross got it out first."

Raven pushed herself up out of the bed. "Speaking of Ross, I want to get this show on the road. After my shower, let's grab something to eat and then head over to meet him."

He grinned. "Once an Alpha, always an Alpha."

She couldn't help but grin back. "Old habits die hard." Passing him, she gave him a cheeky wave and patted his butt. "I'm going to jump in the shower." And she closed the door behind her, but didn't lock it. Being around Simon kept her aroused. Ever hopeful, she thought, shivering deliciously at the idea of sex in the shower.

Inside, her wolf yawned and stretched.

Simon knew he couldn't join her in the shower, though his full erection begged to differ. Instead, he clicked the television back on and got dressed, hoping his arousal would subside by the time Raven finished.

The news program had moved on to something else.

His wolf, always vigilant, had begun to pace. He supposed he could go outside and see if there was a safe area to change, but he didn't want to use the energy. For now, he wanted to focus every fiber of his being on the upcoming confrontation with Ross.

The TV announcer cut in with a break back to the fire at CU. Firefighters had been unable to keep the blaze contained and the conflagration had engulfed several other buildings. Chemicals inside the science labs, the professor's building, had caused several small explosions and police were now evacuating nearby dormitories.

Thus far, they were unaware of any injuries or deaths from this fire.

From the bathroom, the shower cut off. Simon tried like hell not to picture Raven naked, toweling herself dry. Failing completely, his erection surged back full force.

A few minutes later, he heard the blow-dryer.

Finally, Raven emerged, fully clothed. Though she gave him a quizzical look, she said nothing, only coming over to check out the TV. Once again, they were reporting on something else—the stock market and the price of a barrel of crude oil.

Raven smelled of scented lotion. Delicious, he thought, then groaned.

"What's wrong?" she asked.

Wordlessly, he shook his head. As if on cue, his stomach growled.

"I'm hungry, too." Raven laughed. "Are you ready?"

He nodded, struck dumb by her laughter. Standing, he wondered if he could walk. "Give me a minute," he growled. Heading toward the bathroom, he splashed cold water on his face, trying not to notice the fragrant, moisture-scented air.

Once he thought he had himself under control, he rejoined her.

"Let's go."

Outside, the cold air and gray day threatened more snow. Side by side they walked to the motel coffee shop and took a booth. Since the place wasn't crowded, a waitress appeared immediately, brought them coffee and took their order. Both of them ordered steak and eggs.

Though the plates were huge, they both cleaned them. The restaurant clock showed eight-fifteen as he paid the check.

They wheeled the motorcycle outside. She waited while Simon returned the room keys, then they climbed aboard and took off.

In less than thirty minutes, they pulled into a large parking garage.

Once they'd parked and dismounted, Raven

pulled off her helmet and shook her hair free. "Are we there?"

"Next door," Simon said. "This garage is connected by a bridge, though the other side has a guarded gate. Headquarters has restricted entry into their lot. The doors are card-key coded, too."

She frowned. "Why didn't you mention that little detail? How are we going to get in?"

His turn to pull a surprise from his pocket. Grinning, he did just that. "I still have my card. As long as Ross didn't deactivate it, we shouldn't have a problem."

And he was right. On his cell phone on a loud and obviously personal call, the guard at the end of the bridge squinted at Simon's card-key and waved them through impatiently.

At the exterior door, Simon glanced at her. "Now the true test." Sticking his card in the slot, he waited.

The light flashed green. Removing the card, he waited until the door buzzed. "We're in!"

Raven leaned close. "What's the point of all this?"

He shrugged. "Because no one, and I mean no one, has ever even *tried* to breach the Society's headquarters, our security has apparently gotten a little lax."

She raised a brow. "A little?"

Inside, they stood in a lobby. Windowless, locked doors were set in three walls.

"Which one do we want?" she asked.

He pointed. "That one. Let's go."

As he inserted his card, the door buzzed immediately, letting them through. Ahead lay a long hallway punctuated by doors.

"Act like you have a purpose," he whispered to Raven. "Stride though the hall with me as if we're a couple of coworkers here to pick stuff up on our day off. Pretend you belong here."

Immediately, she lifted her chin. Head held high, her expression confident, she transformed into exactly what he'd asked.

In awe, he stared.

"You, too," she ordered, a faint smile on her lips. "And hurry up, someone's coming."

Two men, bent over some papers, approached them.

Simon could only hope they didn't recognize him, or want to talk about one of his recent cases. He wished he had a notebook or clipboard, something he could pretend to discuss with Raven so they wouldn't seem so obvious.

But he'd worried over nothing. Engrossed in their conversation, the two men didn't even glance at them.

"How many floors?" she asked as they approached the elevator. "Are all of these occupied by the Society?"

"Yep. The entire building. Ross's office is on the sixteenth floor." Simon punched the up button. "By the way, there are cameras everywhere. They have an entire floor of people watching monitors. That's the security department."

He grinned. "You might say they're a bit paranoid."

"This seems kind of like the FBI or CIA."

"In a way, it is. The Society is the pack's only intelligence operation. That's why they're so worried about security."

"Aren't you worried?" She glanced at the conspicuous camera over the elevator doors.

"Nah. If they recognize me, they'll only know they've seen me here before. I'm guessing that the only people who know what's going on are those close to Ross. His handpicked team of Protectors."

Though the wait for the elevator seemed to take forever, finally the chime sounded and the door slid open.

They rode to the sixteenth floor in silence, mindful of the ever-present cameras.

Once there, Simon pointed up the corridor. "His office is down there, near the end of the hall."

"Wow." Raven gazed around, her expression stunned. "This is one endless hallway punctuated with doors. Don't they have any open areas?"

"Sure. There is a gym and a cafeteria, as well as a bunch of meeting rooms. Every floor has a couple of those."

She nodded.

"Are you ready?" He didn't take her arm, wanting both hands to be free, just in case. The fact that no one seemed to be in this hall didn't escape his notice. He'd spent quite a bit of time here and couldn't remember the floor ever appearing so deserted.

After glancing in several of the offices as they walked past and noticing they were also empty, a niggling sense of doubt began to bother him.

Had Ross somehow figured out their plan? Were they walking into an elaborate trap? The next second, he shook his head. No way. While Ross might run his own department with an iron fist, no way could he have involved the entire building.

Finally, they reached Ross's office. The door was closed.

Simon glanced once more at Raven. She looked back at him, her gaze steady, then dipped her chin in a quick nod.

He turned the knob and opened the door.

Ross's big chair faced the window. With his back to the door, he lifted his hand impatiently, signaling them to stop. Engrossed in a phone conversation, he continued talking, never once glancing up to see who would dare to interrupt him in his private sanctuary.

He seemed to have aged years since Simon had last seen him. His dark brown hair, formerly only graying at the temples, was now liberally sprinkled with silver.

They stepped inside. Simon closed the door, wishing the handle had a lock.

Raven made a sound of impatience, shifting her weight from foot to foot.

Her movement caught Ross's attention. Still intent on his call, he finally looked up. His pale eyes widened, the only visible sign of his surprise.

Without even saying goodbye to his caller, he dropped his phone back into the cradle. While he gave a quick glance to Simon, his gaze returned and remained on Raven, traveling up and down her slender body in a way that made Simon want to punch him.

"Surprise," Simon said softly.

"I'm surprised you got in."

"I'm not. I still work here. We decided not to wait for Folsom Field."

"You only brought one?" Ross drawled, leaning back in his chair. Then, before Simon could speak, he continued. "Of course, there's no way you could have gotten the younger one."

Raven stiffened, biting her lip.

"What do you mean?" Simon kept his tone level, all too aware the other man was probably baiting them.

Taking his time answering, Ross stood and stretched. Though he might try to convey supreme indifference, tension radiated from the way he held his shoulders.

As he turned, Simon noticed he wasn't wearing his gun holster, a definite plus for them. Casually, he glanced at the coatrack, seeing Ross's jacket. The holster could be under that.

Or else Ross, believing in his supreme invulnerability, didn't bother wearing one at all.

"What's happened to Cee?" Raven asked,

speaking for the first time. "So help me, if you've hurt her…"

"Cee?" Ross frowned. "You mean the girl? She's in Protector custody, that's all."

"How? She knew you were looking for her. She was taking precautions."

"We decided to continue our search-and-retrieve mission." The smile Ross flashed looked decidedly oily. "And as your friend Simon here can tell you, when we want to find something, we usually do. The girl was brought in at 6:58 a.m. this morning. We caught her trying to break back into the professor's house."

Cee. At Raven's stricken look, Simon bit back a curse. "You're bluffing."

"Am I?" Smile widening, Ross moved closer. "And you know this how?"

Digging his, or rather, Whearley's, cell phone from his pocket, Simon watched the other man while scrolling down to find Cee's number.

"I'm calling her," Simon said. "You'd better hope she answers and tells me she's all right."

But after seven rings, the call went to Cee's voice mail. Simon left a brief message, then dropped the phone back in his pocket.

"That's not unusual. She often doesn't answer her phone. She'll call back."

Shaking his head, Ross chuckled. "She won't unless I tell my men to let her. I'm having her brought here."

"Why?"

"That way I can have both of them in the same place. Before the younger one dies, I want to see them side by side with my own eyes."

"The younger one dies?" Raven stepped forward. "What do you mean? Why do you want to kill us? And don't try and give me that crap about us being Feral, because as you can see, I'm clearly not."

Ross looked at her hard. "You really don't know?"

Slowly, she shook her head. "I don't even know who my parents were."

"The professor had files on them. Massive files, with pictures and everything. I'm guessing he didn't let you see them?"

She shook her head. "No."

"Too bad." He sounded completely insincere. "I guess he felt there wasn't a good reason for you to know."

While still speaking, Ross reached for his

phone. Moving fast, Simon intercepted him, knocking it to the floor.

"No calls."

Glaring at the younger man, Ross ran his hand through his close-cropped, silver-tinged hair. "Fine." He glared at Simon. "This is going to end badly for you."

"Your threats don't scare me. Now tell us why you want Raven and Cee so badly. Did the professor experiment on them or something?"

"You fool. The young one—Cee—*is* the experiment. Professor Hutchins kept meticulous records. He cloned her. Cee is Raven's clone."

Chapter 15

"Cloned her? How is that possible?" Stunned, Raven could only stare. "I know they've cloned sheep and other animals, but not a human."

"You are not entirely human, my dear. You're shifter, part wolf."

As if she didn't know. Ever since they'd snuck into this building, her wolf-self had been battling to break free. Even now she had to fight to keep from lifting one corner of her mouth and revealing her teeth.

"Why?" Simon snarled. "Why would he do such a thing? And how are you involved?"

Ross puffed out his chest. "Who do you think provided the funding?"

"But why? What's the purpose?"

Ross flashed him a smug grin. "You never could see the big picture, Caldwell. Think about this for a moment. If we are successful cloning shifters, we won't have to comb the world looking for Protector candidates. We can breed them."

"Your own indoctrinated army." Shaking his head, Simon appeared puzzled. "There's something ethically wrong with your plan."

"Not really. Right now we have to bring new Protectors here as small children, nurse them through separation anxiety, raise and train them. Sixty-seven percent drop out of the program when they become adults. Another twelve percent flake out after ten or twelve years, like you and Beck did. It's becoming more and more difficult to keep trained Protectors."

"Does Turley know about this?"

Ross looked away for a moment. "Not yet. But he will." The grin came back, triumphant. "I'll be a hero."

Simon grimaced. "Is Turley even aware of how many Ferals are exterminated?"

"He doesn't need to know. That's what I'm

here for, so he won't have to get his hands
dirty."

"You know, when I was in training, rehabilitation was always stressed. It wasn't until I
began fieldwork that the emphasis was placed on
extermination."

"Hey," Ross spread his hands. "Not my fault.
Just think of how safe you kept the world by exterminating so many dangerous Ferals."

"Have you ever compiled reports?" Simon's
flat tone contained a warning. "Checked out the
ratio of killed to rehabilitated? I remember
several guys were always asking about that."

"Yeah, like your pal Beck. Guys who need a
vacation."

Simon shook his head. "The ones who questioned always disappeared. I can't believe I never
saw that."

"Of course you didn't." Ross's smile mocked
him. "You were one of the good ones, the guys
who did their job. You were always so focused on
whatever case you'd been assigned, that you
didn't have time to question."

"Turley doesn't know anything, does he? He
sits up there in his lily-white tower, believing
you're taking care of business the way you're

supposed to. Believing you care about the Protector's Code."

For the first time since they'd burst in on him, Ross fidgeted in his chair. "I do care about the Code. I've even been working on rewrites for it. All of this will be in the report I plan to give to Turley."

"When?"

"All in good time. I'm not ready yet."

"You're not going to tell him. You don't want praise. You want power. You're planning to take Turley's spot."

A faint smile played across Ross's mouth, even as he shook his head. "That's an elected position."

"And elections are this fall." Simon frowned. "I'm sure you're working on rigging those, too."

Raven had heard enough. "I don't really care about your Society's internal politics. If Ccc and I are your shining examples of success, why have you been trying so hard to kill us? That doesn't make sense."

Ross gave her a look so cold, it would have melted permafrost. "You're not a shining example. You're a *Feral*. I don't need you alive. Dead, I can have your bodies analyzed, proof positive that the accomplishment is real."

His callous disregard for life stunned her. But then, the entire concept of *extermination* had seemed wrong from the moment she'd learned about it from Simon.

What was one more death to someone with so many already staining his hands?

"You killed the professor, didn't you?"

Ross laughed, ignoring her. "She's pretty smart, for a Feral." He gave Simon the thumbs-up sign. "Which means the younger one is smart, too."

"She has a name," Simon snarled, his expression black. "She's not a thing, she's a person. Her name is Raven. Use it."

After a moment of silence, Ross chuckled. "You, my friend, have it bad."

"No," Simon growled. "I don't. And I'm not your friend."

"She's a Feral. A wild animal. Don't humanize her. There's no point, especially since you know as well as I do that she must die."

"Why?" Taking a step closer, Raven kept her gaze intent on Ross's face, knowing if he looked closely, he'd see her wolf raging behind her eyes. Wild indeed. "Why did you kill the professor?"

Finally, the other man met her gaze. The hatred

she saw in his eyes nearly made her recoil. Instead, she held her ground.

"I'm exterminating everyone who knows about this little project and won't work with my agenda." Ross sounded annoyed that she'd even asked. "What do you care? He was your oppressor, your captor. I'm sure you wanted him dead, didn't you?"

She ignored the question. "If you're killing everyone who knows anything about your experiment, more people have to die."

"Very good." Eyes narrowed, he applauded. "Your powers of deduction are amazing. Of course more have to die. I don't want to take a chance that Turley will find out before I'm ready for him to know."

Watching the two of them silently, Simon took a step forward. "This doesn't make any sense. Even if you started five or ten years ago, by the time all of your clones grew old enough to become full-fledged Protectors, you'll be an old man."

Ross's laugh chilled Raven to the bone. "Really? How old do you think Cee is?"

"She told us. She's nineteen."

"No. She *thinks* she's nineteen. She's actually

only been alive for seven years. The professor cloned her right before you vanished."

Stunned, Raven stared at the pudgy man, hoping she could convey her loathing with a look. "How is that possible?"

"I have legions of scientists around the world." He sounded smug. "Cloning is only one of the projects they're working on for me."

"Working for the Society, you mean," Simon put in. "They're not supposed to be working on your private projects."

"I *am* the Society." Ross stood and yawned. "My projects ultimately benefit them. Now, I think this discussion is just about over."

Without warning, Ross lunged for his desk drawer. Simon leaped. Ross only had the drawer halfway open when Simon hit him, knocking him away. They crashed into Ross's chair on their way to the ground.

Rolling, snarling, they fought. Several times, Raven caught glimpses of wolf, then man, though no one physically changed. The clatter should have been enough to alert someone, but no one came.

Keeping her eye on the two battling men, Raven crossed to the front of the desk. Heart pounding, she reached for the phone and punched zero. When the building operator answered, she asked for Mr. Turley, hoping the other woman didn't notice how her voice shook. To Raven's relief, the call was put through without questions.

A secretary answered, of course. Trying to talk over the sounds of the two men fighting, Raven attempted to tell the woman she had a matter of extreme security to discuss with Mr. Turley. As the woman attempted to deflect her, Raven told her in a flat voice to tell Mr. Turley if he wanted to keep the building from exploding, he needed to go to Ross's office on the sixteenth floor. Immediately.

Then, her piece said, Raven hung up. Now all she had to do was pray the secretary would relay her message. A bomb threat should be enough to get even the great man's attention. At the very least, it would buy them some time.

Now if she could just keep Simon and his former boss from killing each other. As long as she remained human, there seemed little danger of that, thank goodness.

If everything went well, soon she and Simon would be free of this mess. If not...they'd probably both soon be dead.

With a sigh, she turned around just in time to see Simon clock Ross with a well-timed punch.

The older man's head shot back, into the corner of the credenza, knocking him out.

Bleeding from a cut on his lip, Simon climbed slowly to his feet. "What did you just do?" he croaked, motioning at the phone.

"I called Turley. He has a right to know. I refuse to be in the middle of a power struggle between him—" she jerked her thumb toward Ross "—and his higher-up."

"For all you know he could be in on it," Simon snarled. "But you said—"

"I know what I said. Now I'm thinking we would have been better off taking our chances."

He barely got out the last word when the door burst open. Armed security guards rushed into the room, shouting at them to put their hands up.

Moving slowly and carefully even though her heart pounded so hard she thought it might burst from her chest, Raven did as they asked.

"I think something went wrong," Simon said low-voiced as he was cuffed. "Turley didn't bother coming. Either he didn't get the message or…"

Shaking her head, Raven finished his sentence for him. "Or Turley doesn't care. Turley doesn't care at all."

As they started to lead Simon away, Raven started after him.

"No." One of the uniformed officers blocked her. "You'll be questioned separately."

Made sense, sort of. Gazing after Simon until he turned the corner, she glanced back over her shoulder, watching as paramedics tended to a groggy Ross. As soon as he could speak coherently, she had no doubt he'd spin some fantastic story about a crazed former Protector and his Feral, out for revenge.

Of course, she should have known. Her past experience had proved books and movies were wrong. Good didn't always triumph over evil. In her life at least, bad people always seemed to win.

Just once, she'd have liked to have seen things end differently. Now, if Ross had his way, she'd never have a second chance. She and Simon would never have a chance.

Or Cee. Or Beck. Or Zach. Even poor Theo, who'd done nothing more wrong than follow his pack leader, would die.

This strengthened her resolve. No way would she go down without a fight.

Instead of taking her to a prison cell or some windowless, locked room, the instant her two guards turned the corner, they headed toward the elevators.

"Don't worry," one of them said. "You're safe."

The other frowned in disapproval, but didn't dispute his partner's statement.

At the landing, the silent guard used a key to activate an elevator marked *Private*. The doors slid soundlessly open, revealing an interior paneled in polished mahogany and floored in thick, burgundy carpet.

Inside, instead of a multibutton panel, there was only one button, rimmed in antique brass. The guard pressed once and the elevator began gliding upward, finally coming to a smooth stop.

As the doors opened and they moved forward, Raven realized they'd entered an entirely different world. Where the other part of the building looked like a standard government office, strictly utilitarian, this floor appeared as luxuriously appointed as the penthouse suite of a high-end resort hotel.

Flanked by her guards, they walked the length of the large waiting room. Furnished with elegant couches and chairs, the focal point of the room appeared to be a huge, L-shaped, cherrywood desk. A tall, elegant woman in a dark-colored, tailored suit and stiletto heels waited there.

Though she nodded at the two security guards, she smiled at Raven before addressing them. "Release her."

Once they'd unlocked her cuffs, she nodded. "Please come with me."

After a quick glance at her escorts, ascertaining they meant to stay behind, Raven followed the woman through a set of doors, entered and exited another room, then another, making her feel like a mouse caught in an elegant maze. At the final door, an ornately carved wooden panel decorated with mythic figures and wolves, the woman smiled once more and dipped her chin.

"From here, you must go alone." She indicated the door. "Go ahead. It's not locked."

Heart pounding, Raven summoned a smile and grasped the handle. Pulling, she opened the door and entered the room.

And came face-to-face with a huge wolf with a coat so purely white, it appeared to glow.

Frozen, puzzling over this development, the air around the animal shimmered and sparkled. Raven blinked, suppressing the urge to rub her eyes. An instant later, a white-haired man stood naked in front of her.

Giving her a serene smile, he turned and pulled on a pair of jeans and a shirt that had been draped over one of the two plush chairs.

"Please, sit." He indicated the other chair. Waiting until she was seated, he dropped into the one across from her and held out his hand. "I'm Geoff Turley, head of the Society. Rest assured, I'm aware of Ross's plans and know what he's trying to do."

Refusing to take his hand, she glared at him. "Were you aware how many Fer—er, wild wolves he's slated for extermination?"

Sadness filled his large gray eyes. "Recently, I learned about this, yes. My intelligence has been faulty. They focused too much on the big picture and not enough on the little."

"So what are you going to do about it?"

If her forthrightness surprised him, he gave no sign. "I've already ordered a recall of all Protectors in the field. They'll all go through retraining. We're here to protect, not to destroy."

"And if a wild shifter doesn't want to be rehabilitated, what then? Will you still order death?"

He sighed. "These things are complicated. Some of them are mad, a danger to themselves and others. When one kills a human, we have to take great pains to make certain the truth isn't discovered. Some of those are beyond even our best attempts at rehabilitation."

With a dip of her chin, she conceded that point. "But there are others, like me, who just want to live their lives and be left alone. What about them?"

"That's what a Protector is supposed to do. Assess the threat. Someone like you—clearly intelligent, with access to society, yet who lives wild by choice—should be free to do as they please."

"What about Simon?"

"Your mate? He will be informed. After the conclusion of this investigation, you will be free to live as you wish."

"I don't understand," she said slowly. "What do you mean, my mate?"

He gave her a smile tinged with sadness. "Like our wild counterparts, shifters mate only once. When we find that special person, our mate, the joy we experience in our union knows no bounds."

"And you?" She kept her voice soft. "Have you found your mate?"

"I did, yes." His voice thickened and grief clouded his eyes. "We were married twelve years.

I lost her in a house fire, seven years ago. Even now, I find it difficult to talk about."

Though words weren't adequate, she did the best she could. "I'm so sorry."

"Don't be," he said quietly. "I wouldn't have traded those years of happiness for not experiencing this pain... If you feel that Simon is your mate, don't let him get away without telling him."

Though she nodded and managed what she hoped was a convincing smile, his words only brought more pain. Even if she believed they were mates, someone like Simon would never want someone like her—a castaway. A Feral.

"Tell him," Turley urged.

"I will. Where is he now?"

"I've also ordered him brought to me." He glanced at a huge wall clock with Roman numerals. "I expect him at any moment."

Led away in handcuffs, Simon kept glancing over his shoulder as Raven was taken away in the opposite direction. He would do whatever was necessary to ensure her survival, even if he had to sacrifice his own life. No way would he let harm come to his mate.

His mate.

Finally, he could acknowledge the truth. Raven and he were mates, a fated pair, meant to be together. Living the rest of his life by her side was the only way he wanted to live.

First opportunity he got, he was busting out of here and going for her.

His two guards led him to the stairwell, making him wonder if they planned to toss him down several floors to his death. Instead, they prodded him upward. One more floor. Two. As they rounded the corner of the nineteenth floor, Simon noticed his escorts appeared to be growing winded. The one on his left, a good fifty pounds overweight, wheezed and gasped for air. The one on the right, slightly younger and in a bit better shape, was out of breath.

Simon hid a savage grin. Sometimes he knew he had to make his own opportunities.

He took one now, elbowing the guard on the left, then as the man doubled over, shoving him into the one on the right. Not watching to see how far they fell, he took off, taking the stairs two and three at a time.

Behind him, he could hear his guards struggling to catch up.

This building had twenty-one floors. Turley's

offices occupied the entire top floor. If he could get to Turley, he and Raven might have a chance. Otherwise, they were as good as dead.

He could only hope once he got to the twenty-first floor, he wouldn't find the stairwell doorway locked.

His luck held. Panting only slightly, hearing the guards struggling up a floor below him, he grasped the doorknob and turned. The door opened. Stepping inside, Simon turned the lock, effectively halting his pursuers. They'd have to go back to the twentieth floor and see if they could find someone with a key to use the private elevator. Even if they did, Simon had just bought himself enough time to do what he needed.

No one stopped him, not in the plush waiting room, nor the antechambers after. Finally, he reached the big man's office, the ornate door carved with symbols of power. Taking a deep breath, Simon burst through the door, ready to do battle.

Instead, he found himself facing Raven and Turley, sitting across from each other in comfortable chairs, looking at him and smiling.

Later, after Turley listened and explained the immediate changes he'd ordered, they learned

Ross had been led away to be brought up on charges. The counts against him were so numerous they took up three single-spaced pages.

Cee, Beck and Zach had all been released. Simon and Raven were free to go, though Simon had been ordered back to active duty in two weeks' time. Like all the other Protectors who'd served under Ross, he would have to undergo extensive retraining.

Finally, as they got up to leave, Simon took Raven's hand.

"Wait," Turley said. "Raven has told me she wants her life back the way it was before. She isn't a danger to anyone. I have one final order. Before you start your two-week leave, return her to the place where you found her."

He appeared to be watching closely for a reaction, even as he clapped Simon hard on the back. "Then we can all live happily ever after, eh?"

Stunned, Simon managed to nod.

The head of the Society leaned close, speaking in a low voice so only he could hear. "Are you aware of the possibility she may be your mate?"

Simon swallowed. Jerking his head in what amounted to a nod, he met the other man's gaze. "Yes," he answered. "Yes, I am."

Turley nodded, releasing him. "Then you're free to go."

Shell-shocked, Simon turned blindly, reaching for Raven. Maybe he'd known all along, somewhere deep inside him, that she was his mate. But did she?

As their hands connected, he found himself searching her face for an answer. Unaware of his thoughts, she gave him a reassuring smile.

"Are you ready?"

"Yes." Chest tight, he held on to Raven's hand until they made it to the elevator, then released her.

He should have known this moment would come. He had to let her go.

On the elevator ride down, she gave him a tired smile. "I've got to figure out what to tell Cee," she said. "I'm not sure if I want her to know anything about cloning, yet I have to tell her we're family."

He nodded, knowing he couldn't speak, not yet. Not until he wrapped his mind around the idea of a life without her. Part of him kept hoping she'd refute Turley's words, tell him she didn't want to return to her mountain, even though all along she'd told Simon the same thing.

She wanted to go home.

He would give her what she wanted.

The motorcycle sat parked exactly where they'd left it. Simon handed Raven her helmet, buckling his own and swallowing to clear his aching throat.

"Do you mind if we stop to check on Theo?" Her clear blue gaze contained no hint of her thoughts.

"Sure," he managed, climbing on the bike and waiting for her. "No problem."

The two-hour drive back to Boulder passed in a blur.

At the clinic, they found Zach, looking well rested.

"Are you okay?" Simon clasped his friend's arm. "I was worried about you."

"Fine." Zach grinned. "They asked a few questions, kept me locked in a room in the Lamplighter Motel. Finally, one of my guards got a phone call and they let me go."

"How's Theo?" Raven could scarcely contain herself. "Is his leg healing?"

"You know I had to amputate, right?"

She nodded.

"He's healing well, though it'll be awhile before he'll be able to walk again. He'll have to be caged for a few more days. Are you planning on releasing him into the wild?"

Frowning, she bit her lip. "I don't know. He was never one of the strong ones in the pack, and he's so young."

"There's a wolf refuge north of here, up near Fort Collins. I can make a call and see if they'll take him."

"Would you?" Her entire face lit up, making Simon's chest ache again. Even Zach appeared entranced as he slowly nodded.

"Can I see him?"

"Sure." Zach led her away, returning a moment later alone. "What happened to you, man?" he asked softly. "You look like you got run over by a truck."

Rubbing the back of his neck, Simon shook his head. "Nothing time and a fifth of whiskey won't cure."

The wolf sanctuary could take Theo in a couple of weeks. Until then, he'd have to remain in Raven and Simon's care. Since Simon was still staying with Zach, the vet agreed to keep him at the clinic, as long as he wasn't a danger to any of his employees.

It turned out the professor had willed Cee his house near the Hill. Raven went to stay with her for a few days, leaving Simon alone. And miserable.

He tried to tell himself the absence would be good practice for when Raven left for good, but nothing worked. He lost count of how many times he had to stop himself from calling her and when he caught himself turning down Cee's street, he realized he'd turned into a basket case.

Even changing didn't help. Driving up into the mountains to let his wolf run free only reminded him of Raven's absence.

Mates weren't meant to be separated.

He wondered if Raven was as miserable as he, or if he'd gotten the mate thing completely wrong. Finally, he gave in to impulse and called her.

Cee answered. "Hey, Simon. We found a box of photos of Raven and my parents. They're awesome! You should come by and check them out. We look just like our mom."

Which meant Raven had told her. "I'll do that, soon. Is Raven around?"

"She's out somewhere. I think she might have gone hiking. Do you want me to have her call you?"

Torn, he finally told Cee he'd call back later, knowing he wouldn't. When he hung up, he had to battle the urge to comb the hiking trails near her house in search of her.

When Zach told him a week later that Theo

had grown strong enough to be taken to the sanctuary, Simon jumped at the chance to call Raven. Hearing her voice sent a chill down his spine.

Though she sounded happy to hear from him, she didn't sound as if she'd experienced anything like the desperation coiling inside him. He agreed to pick her up in the morning for breakfast, after which they'd go get Theo and take him up to Fort Collins.

The next morning, though he tried to prepare himself, he went weak in the knees at his first sight of Raven. She came to the door in a bright yellow, cable-knit sweater and jeans, her long hair tied up in a jaunty ponytail. He got out of Zach's SUV, holding on to the side for balance, and attempted a casual wave and an even more casual smile.

But Raven would have none of that. Grinning, she barreled down the sidewalk and jumped into his arms. Wrapping her legs around his waist, she kissed his neck, his cheek, even his nose, before finally reaching his lips.

Blood thundering, he held her, letting himself sink into the kiss. When she finally broke away, laughing and breathless, he carefully placed her on her feet and prayed she didn't notice his arousal.

"Hellhounds, that felt good," he said, before thinking better of it.

"Sure did." She leaned in and gave him one more quick kiss before going around to the other side of the SUV. "I'm so glad you're here."

He felt a flush of pleasure. "Me, too." Understatement of the year.

"Cee will be disappointed she missed you." Buckling her seat belt, she grinned. "When I told her how we're related, I thought she might take it badly, but we found a couple of boxes of old pictures. That helped."

"Are you two close now?" he asked, unable to tear his gaze away from her.

"Sure." Her grin widened. "We're only seven years apart and closer than most sisters. After all, she *is* a clone of me."

"I'm glad you finally told her."

"Yeah. Finding those old photos really was something. Seeing my parents, our parents, after all these years helped heal my heart." She sighed. "But you know what? Cee is great and all, but I really want my normal life back."

Her normal life. Just like that, the joy went out of his day. As Turley had said, she was entitled to return to the life she'd lived before. Before him.

She was right to remind him. Hell, he'd reminded himself a hundred times on the way over to pick her up.

But he'd been unable to quash the small, niggling hope that upon seeing him she'd realize they were mates and decide she wanted him more.

Zach had sedated Theo and had three assistants help them load the caged wolf into the back of the SUV.

Simon thanked him and waved goodbye, but instead of heading north, he drove west, into the mountains. Though most of the high passes were closed for the winter, he figured he could get close enough to do what he needed to do. Set her free.

At a scenic overlook, he pulled the SUV over.

"What's wrong?" Raven sounded puzzled. "Are you having car trouble?"

"No." He gestured upward, toward the snow-covered peaks and rugged terrain. "I came here first so I could give you what you wanted, before I completely lost all my willpower."

Staring at him, she bit her lip. "I'm not sure I understand."

"Go," he told her, somehow managing to smile while his heart felt as if it was splitting in two.

"We're close enough to your old cave. I can let you both go and Theo will help you find it."

Silent, she continued to watch him, a shadow darkening her eyes to the color of dusk.

He forced a smile. "I'm sure if you return to the same general area, you can find your old pack of wild wolves. Though you might have to fight Mandy again for the Alpha spot." His stupid, insincere smile wavered as he pictured her battling the she-wolf.

"Go," he said again. "Go."

She didn't move. "Why?" she asked softly. "Why are you pushing me away?"

"This is what you want, right?" Without waiting for an answer, he continued, flinching inwardly at the bitterness in his voice. "All I can do is give you what you want, what you've asked for all along. Your old life, your freedom."

She unfastened her seat belt, sending a flutter of panic through his chest. "You're letting me go?"

"I'm giving you what you asked for. Your happiness."

"And you think this is what I would like?"

"Isn't it? This is what you've told me all along. Even today, when I picked you up, you said you wanted your normal life back." His voice broke.

Doggedly, he forced himself to continue. "I don't want you to go. If it were up to me..." He didn't dare finish, mostly because he knew he couldn't.

"If it were up to you?"

He shook his head. "Raven, don't you see? All along, I'd hoped that once this was over, I'd be able to give you what you needed. That I would be enough for you. That together, we could make our own happiness."

"Ah, Simon." Her soft smile felt like a gut punch. Though he searched her eyes, he found no pity in her gaze. When she reached out and laid her hand along the curve of his jaw, it took everything inside him not to flinch away. "Do you promise?"

"Promise?" He rasped the word.

"To love me as much as I love you. Forever."

His throat appeared to have closed, and now all he could do was jerk his head in a nod, scarcely able to believe, hardly able to breathe.

"Then, I'll tell you what I want." She came closer, so close their bodies nearly touched. So close he had to clench his hands into fists to keep from touching her.

"I want you," she told him. "Only you."

Leaning over, she slanted her mouth over his for a deep, soul-shattering kiss.

He kissed her back, fighting with himself, juggling joy, incredulity and stubborn disbelief. And fear, most of all fear. That he could actually envision such happiness, such complete and utter joy, and then learn it wasn't meant to be.

Confused, he didn't understand. She wanted to live as a wild wolf, head of her wild pack in the wilderness, didn't she?

As if she'd read his mind, she shook her head. "Not anymore," she told him. "Not without you."

At first, the words didn't register. When they did, the tightness in his chest eased somewhat.

"Why?" One word was all he could manage.

"Because I love you. You're my mate." Her brilliant smile took his breath away, as did her second kiss, and her third.

Once he could breathe again, he held her, feeling as though the earth spun wildly, ground shifting under his feet. There should be fireworks, he thought. Trumpets blaring, clouds parting, rainbows.

Even as he lifted his gaze, waiting, a stray sunbeam fought its way through the clouds, lighting up Raven's mountain as though by spotlight.

"There." She pointed, gazing up at the peak as though she'd once again read his mind. "There's your sign."

He didn't bother to ask her what she meant. They both knew. Raven. His mate, his love.

She loved him. He could scarcely take it all in.

She raised her head, studying his face, her own expression serious. "Commonly, the person being told I love you should say it back." A flash of doubt crossed her beautiful face. "Unless…"

"Don't even think that." Finally, at last, he could give her this. He could tell her how he felt. Though a simple thing, these were words he'd never said to anyone, anytime, anyplace.

He cleared his throat. "I love you," he said. Then, because his voice sounded rusty, he said them again. "I love you, Raven. You're my mate. Forever and always."

With a sigh, she melted into him and kissed him again.

Drowning in her, he managed to pull back. This was too important. There could be no misunderstanding or questions or doubt. "Raven, are you sure? You know we can't live in a cave up in the mountains?"

Only love blazed from her impossibly blue eyes. "I know. And I still love you." One corner of her mouth lifted. "Before you ask again, yes, I'm positive."

"Even if you have to spend a good deal of your time living among humans?"

She grinned. "Even if. As long as I have you by my side, and we change often, I'm good."

"And Theo," he reminded her, indicating the huge, yellow-eyed wolf, still unconscious in the cage. "You could keep him for a pet, if you like."

"No. I wouldn't do that to him. He'll do well at the sanctuary. He'll find a new pack, maybe even a mate." She moved back to her seat and fastened the belt. "We'd better get him there before the sedative wears off."

Reluctant to let go of her, nonetheless he put the SUV in Drive and began turning around, to go back into town and pick up the highway north into Fort Collins.

"On the way there," she flashed an impish grin that warmed him all the way to his feet, "we can discuss where we want to live. I'd like to live close to the mountains."

"Is that all?" he teased, loving her so much it hurt.

Gazing up at him through her lashes, she took

a deep breath. "No. My one other requirement is a good school district for our children."

Children. With her words, his last shred of doubt vanished. They'd have children, make a family of their own.

As the road curved to reveal Boulder spread out below them, the clouds once again parted, bathing the sprawling city in bright sunlight. Taking a deep breath, Simon realized his future, their future, contained endless possibilities for happiness, joy and more. A wealth of emotion, all waiting to be experienced.

And love of course. Always love, with his wild wolf mate right by his side.

* * * * *

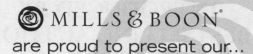

MILLS & BOON

are proud to present our...

Book of the Month

The Baby Gift
A beautiful linked duet
by Alison Roberts from
Mills & Boon® Medical™

WISHING FOR A MIRACLE

Mac MacCulloch and Julia Bennett make the perfect team. But Julia knows she must protect her heart – especially as she can't have children. She's stopped wishing for a miracle, but Mac's wish is standing right in front of him – Julia…and whatever the future may hold.

THE MARRY-ME WISH

Paediatric surgeon Anne Bennett is carrying her sister's twins for her when she bumps into ex-love Dr David Earnshaw! When the babies are born, learning to live without them is harder than Anne ever expected – and she discovers that she needs David more than ever…

Mills & Boon® Medical™
Available 6th August

Something to say about our
Book of the Month?
Tell us what you think!
millsandboon.co.uk/community

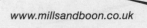

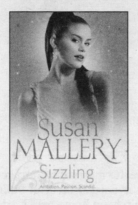

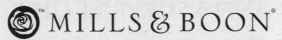

FREE BOOK
AND A SURPRISE GIFT

We would like to take this opportunity to thank you for reading this Mills & Boon® book by offering you the chance to take A specially selected book from the Nocturne series absolutely FREE! We're also making this offer to introduce you to the benefits of the Mills & Boon® Book Club™—

- **FREE home delivery**
- **FREE gifts and competitions**
- **FREE monthly Newsletter**
- **Exclusive Mills & Boon Book Club offers**
- **Books available before they're in the shops**

Accepting this FREE book and gift places you under no obligation to buy, you may cancel at any time, even after receiving your free book. Simply complete your details below and return the entire page to the address below. You don't even need a stamp!

YES Please send me a free Nocturne book and a surprise gift. I understand that unless you hear from me, I will receive 3 superb new stories every month, two priced at £4.99 and a third larger version priced at £6.99, postage and packing free. I am under no obligation to purchase any books and may cancel my subscription at any time. The free book and gift will be mine to keep in any case.

Ms/Mrs/Miss/Mr _____ Initials _____

_____

Surname _____

Address _____

_____ Postcode _____

E-mail _____

Send this whole page to: Mills & Boon Book Club, Free Book Offer, FREEPOST NAT 10298, Richmond, TW9 1BR